DARK PLACES

A MARK HAYES STORY

BRENT TOWNS

ROUGH
EDGES
PRESS

Dark Please
Paperback Edition

Rough Edges Press
An Imprint of Wolfpack Publishing
9850 S. Maryland Parkway, Suite A-5 #323
Las Vegas, Nevada 89183

roughedgespress.com

Paperback ISBN 978-1-68549-211-3
eBook ISBN 978-1-68549-210-6
LCCN 2022948935

DARK PLACES

CHAPTER ONE

Friar's Lake

I stared hard at the thief who stood before me. His eyes narrowed and I knew I was in for a rough time. "I saw you take it," I said.

"Bugger off," came the terse reply. "I didn't take nothing."

"You're just going to stand there and lie to my face even though I saw you?"

"Just because you're a private investigator doesn't mean you're shit hot," he shot back at me.

He was right, I was a private investigator, but he was wrong about one thing. I *was* shit hot. The sun outside the shop was beating down something terrible and the tar on the street was liquefying. So much so that every time a car drove past you could hear the tread unsticking itself with each wheel turn.

The takeaway shop we were in had no air-conditioning and touching the stainless-steel countertop would lead to a second-degree burn.

"Mark, leave it," the lady behind the counter said to me. That was my name. Mark Hayes.

I glanced at her. Elvira Woods was an elderly woman who'd owned the Beef and Burger Takeaway for the best part of ten years. Her gray hair had a tinge of purple, remnant of her last rinse almost a month ago. She was due for the hairdresser again this week.

Shaking my head, I said, "No, Elvira. You give them an inch and they take a mile."

"It wasn't much."

"That is not the point. It's the principle."

"Get out of my way, asshole," the thief growled at me.

I glanced at the woman behind the counter, shaking my head. "Total lack of respect."

"Can I help here?" a female voice asked from behind me where I stood blocking the doorway. "Mark, get out of the way."

I stepped to one side and let the woman through. She was dressed in a police uniform with sergeant stripes on the epaulettes. I stared at the thief and said, "You're screwed now."

Sergeant Nicole Berger stopped beside me. Not only was she Friar's Lake's senior police person, she was also my lover. Can you say that? Lover? Or maybe it's partner.

She was my age, in her mid-thirties. Her hair was dark, and as usual, she wore it in a bun when working. Her uniform was dark. Navy pants, navy shirt. She stared at me with her dark eyes and said, "Do you want to tell me what is going on?"

I nodded. "Swifty here was stealing. I saw him doing it."

She glared at the thief. "Is that true?"

"No."

"Turn out your pockets."

"Got a warrant?"

"I don't need a warrant, now turn them out."

"It's all right," Elvira said. "It wasn't much."

Nicole looked at her. "Are you sure?"

She nodded. "Yes, it's not worth the hassle."

I saw Nicole shrug and then she said, "All right, get out of here."

Eight-year-old Tommy Hansen dived for the doorway and disappeared through the streamer curtain used to keep the flies out of the café. Nicole smiled at me. "The big bad PI been picking on the town kids again?"

"Not the point."

"Yeah, well, wait until he gets home and tells his father."

I rolled my eyes. Bomber Hansen was a thug. There was no other way to describe him. He'd only been back in town for three months after his release from prison and was already causing trouble. "Big prick raising a little prick," I growled.

"Just keep an eye out. Anyway, don't you have anything better to do?"

"If you must know, I was in here ordering lunch so I could eat with you on your break."

"You were?" She looked at me incredulously then stepped over to the drinks fridge and removed a bottle of water.

"Almost."

Nicole frowned at me. "What do you mean, almost?"

"I never quite got there because I caught Ronnie Biggs trying to rob the train."

She chuckled at me. "You exaggerate."

"Tell me that when ten years from now the young punk is holding up the local roadhouse."

She shook her head and looked at Elvira. "Can I order something to eat, please?"

"Sure, sweetie, what'll it be?"

"Salad sandwich. And the water, thanks."

"No problem. What about Jim Rockford?"

I thought about shooting back a retort but instead said, "Pie, chips, and a Coke. Thank you."

"Real healthy, Mark," Nicole said.

"I'd rather it be beer, but I'd probably melt before I got to the pub."

Nicole and I sat down outside while we waited for the food. Crazy, you might say, but it didn't matter. Inside, outside, it was all just as hot. Outside, however, held the added bonus of flies. "You been busy this morning?"

She rolled her eyes. I liked it when she did that; there was something about it which made me want to take her to bed when it happened. She said, "Sure, Friar's Lake is just a hotbed of sin and illegal activity."

"Do tell."

"All right. First, there was a missing cat. Mavis Burgess had me out looking for it for an hour before I found it."

"Down a drain?" I asked.

"Dead in the gutter a block from where she lives."

"Dogs?"

"Dunlop radial."

I winced. "Oh."

"Next, I got a call about a flasher at the nursing home. I took Jace with me and found Jack Perkins sitting on a bench seat in a raincoat stroking his Johnson for the world to see."

I chuckled.

"Not funny," Nicole growled. "It was a damned circus. Them old girls were behaving like drunk teenagers out underage drinking, egging him on."

I gave her a sly glance. "Well hung?"

"Like a fucking horse." It was her turn to laugh now.

"They say when you get older things droop or get smaller. Not in his case."

"Anything else?" I asked her.

A small look of surprise came to her face. "There was one thing. Pru Jacobs would like to hire your services."

"What for?"

"Someone stole her cooler."

It was my turn to roll my eyes. "You've got to be kidding me."

"Hey, don't complain, it's work."

"I'm too busy."

"Bullshit. You've got one other case on," Nicole shot back at me. She nudged me. "Maybe they're related."

I shook my head. "How can a stolen cooler be related to Deadhead Dave's suspicions that his wife is screwing his best mate."

"Is she?" she asked as she put her bottle of water up to her lips for a drink.

I shook my head. "No, she's screwing his brother."

Nicole snorted water from her nose and mouth and began a coughing fit, almost drowning herself. Some of it splashed onto the dusty footpath while the rest spilled down her uniform. "Shit a brick," she growled. "You need to warn me about stuff like that."

"Yeah, well…"

"When are you going to tell him?"

"Maybe tomorrow. I need to get some pictures first to back up my story. I don't think I'll go chasing the nasty evidence. Photos will suffice."

"How will you do that?"

"It's Dave's bingo night. While he's out I'd bet my left nut that his brother will come calling."

"Just be careful," Nicole cautioned him. "Getting mixed up in family shit can be dangerous."

"Not as dangerous as this is about to get," I replied, nodding to indicate something along the street.

"What?" she asked and turned to look in that direction then swore. "Shit, I knew this was going to happen."

Through the shimmering heat haze rising from the dirty main street of Friar's Lake walked a large man. His head was shaved, there were holes in his jeans, and his shirt had had the sleeves ripped out to reveal muscular arms sporting tattoos.

Bomber Hansen was a big man who looked mean at the best of times, but right at that moment, appeared to be somewhat aggro. Nicole said as she stood to face him, "You want me to shoot him before he gets here?"

That would be nice, thanks. "No, I can handle it."

I stood up as well.

"Good luck."

The man seemed to get larger with proximity.

Looking around I realized there wasn't much that could be used as a weapon. Let's face it, the guy would probably kick the shit out of me if I didn't have something to protect myself with. "Can I have your taser, Nicole?"

"No."

"Glock?"

"Pussy."

"If I die here, will you come to my funeral?"

She grinned. "I'll even lay across your coffin, sobbing like a distraught wife."

"You got to be married to do that."

"Was that a proposal, Mark?"

I snorted. "The hell it was."

I'd been married once before. A lovely lass named Tia. She was a cop, too, a Homicide detective. Wonderful woman she was. The girl of my dreams, until she wasn't. Things crumbled and divorce followed. I'd been a cop, too, at one time. Then things happened and I was kicked off the force. That was when I became a private investigator in Melbourne. Overall, it wasn't a bad job, but things occasionally became interesting in the not necessarily fun kind of way.

That was how I met Nicole. I had been looking for a missing person and got mixed up in a drug smuggling operation as well as hunting a serial killer. By the time it was all wrapped up, there were too many dead, including Nicole's old boss, Sergeant Tomika Rains.

As soon as Bomber was within reach his deep voice growled, "You the prick who said my boy was stealing?"

I nodded. "Yeah."

"Did you give him a clip under the ear?"

"Didn't get a chance."

He spat on the ground at his feet and his eyes narrowed. "Next time belt his ass. Little shit ought to know better."

"I'll do that."

The big man turned and stalked away.

I looked at Nicole. "Well, what about that?"

She grinned at me. "Must be your lucky day."

"Want to go home for lunch?" I raised an eyebrow suggestively.

"You're not that lucky, Champ." She laughed.

No harm in trying. My hang dog look didn't need to be feigned.

Pru Jacobs was a woman in her early sixties. Her gray hair shone with a blue hue from a recent rinse, and her a face was like a desert plain after a good storm which left great washes gouged out. She saw me coming up the sidewalk towards the front door doing my best to avoid falling to my death in the gigantic cracks in the concrete.

She opened the door and waved at me, smiling.

"Hello, Mark. Glad you could come. Nicole said you'd be able to help."

"I'll try, Pru. Although I should tell you up front that finding lost household items isn't what I normally do."

"I know, that's why I'm so appreciative that you came. Please, come inside."

I walked up the steps and in through the door. The first thing I noticed was the smell. It was an odor I'd smelled many times over the years. It's the smell that permeates homes where old people reside. Mothballs, camphor, age—*eau de aging*.

"Would you like a cup of tea, dear?" she asked me.

"No, thanks, Pru. I've not long had lunch."

"Oh. I bet it was nice and healthy, a strapping young man like yourself. What was it? Salad? Fruit? Smoothie?"

Pie, chips, Coke. "All of the above, Pru."

"I knew it." She sounded so proud and gave a little grin.

"Where did they take the cooler from, Pru?"

Smiling again, she said, "Follow me."

I followed her along the hallway and out through the kitchen to the back door. We went out and the flyscreen door slammed shut behind us. Her yard was desperate for a good water, but that was in short supply at the moment and most of the lawns around the town sported similar shades of brown.

"It was right there, Mark," she said, pointing at a place near the rear wall of the house. "It was there yesterday but gone this morning."

I looked around. The gate had a padlock which was intact, and the fence was relatively high so anyone who jumped it would not be visible to neighbors. And the only way someone could know of its presence was if they had been to the house recently. "Was it a good cooler, Pru?"

She shook her head. "No. But it was still all right. But that's not it. They had to have climbed my fence to get it. What if I'd have caught them?"

"I hear you. What would you like me to do?"

"Find them and take them to your wife."

I was grinning on the inside imagining Nicole's retort. "She's not my wife."

"Oh, but I thought…"

I shook my head. "Nope."

"Oh, dear."

She turned red and her mouth opened and closed like a caught bass. "Ah, how much do you want?" she asked, changing the subject.

"I tell you what, why don't we discuss money once I find it."

"Okay. Now, you better come back inside."

"All right."

Returning to her sitting room, she picked up something off the side table. She held it out to me, and I frowned. "It's a picture of the cooler. You won't find it if you don't know what it looks like."

"Thank you. There are a couple of questions that I have for you before I go."

She nodded expectantly. "Yes?"

"Has there been anyone here doing work for you over the past few days?"

She looked thoughtful for a moment before stabbing a finger at me and saying, "I did have young Barry Green here the other day."

"Who is Barry Green?"

"He does air conditioners. Mine was playing up so I called him."

"Where is the unit?" I asked her.

"Out the back."

"Right, anyone else?"

"Oh, yes. Jim Kelly the plumber. It's been a bad week. He did some unblocking work out the back as well."

"Same day?"

"Same time actually."

There we are. I had two suspects already and couldn't work out why either of them would steal a used cooler. "Thank you, Pru. I'll see what I can do."

She walked me to the front door and waved to me as I left. Now I had two choices of what to do. I could go back to Nicole's, take my clothes off and enjoy the air conditioning, or I could go and see some blokes about a cooler. The sun beat down, the flies were a thick black cloud, and —bugger it, I had other work to do. I went back to Nicole's.

Surprisingly, Nicole was there when I arrived. She was parading around in a black thong and a white T-shirt, enjoying the coolness of the air conditioning. "Expecting me, were you?" I asked with a grin.

"No, I was actually expecting my other lover."

I took her in my arms and kissed her. Her hair was still wet from the cool shower she'd just had, and it told from the touch of her skin when I cupped her buttocks. "Why are you home?"

She grinned and kissed me again. "Just for a quick shower, Romeo, and then back out fighting crime. How did you go with Pru Jacobs?"

I released her and walked over to the refrigerator. "It was either the plumber or the refrigeration mechanic."

Nicole started putting on a fresh uniform. "Really, you solved it that quick?"

I took out a Coke and cracked it. The *shh* of escaping

gas was music to my ears. After a mouthful I said, "Tell me this, who on earth wants to steal a used cooler?"

This time when she smiled, I could see her white teeth. "A plumber or a refrigeration mechanic."

I glared at her, and she pulled a face.

She left her pants open while she put on her shirt. "What time will you be home tonight?"

"I'm not sure. After I get some pictures."

"Peeping Tom."

It was my turn to grin, although mine held no mirth. "I love my job?"

"I was thinking that after we are both finished, we could meet up at the pub?"

"Bingo starts at seven, give his brother time to get over, clothes off, and…yeah should be there by eight."

"You seem awfully confident."

"Trust me, if it's anything like the other night the front curtains will be open, and the world will be watching them on stage."

Nicole raised her eyebrows. "Seriously?"

"Yes, I don't even know why he hired me. The whole of Friar's Lake knows."

"I didn't."

"Yeah, but you're a police officer. You're always the last to know anything."

Once her shoes went on, she followed with her belt, and Nicole was ready to return to work. She came over to me, kissed my lips once more and said, "See you tonight, Rockford."

"You wish."

"Mmm, he was a handsome man."

"Bitch."

"Bye."

"See you."

The door closed and she was gone. Now it was my

turn for a three-minute shower. Three minutes? It would rain one day.

Deadhead Dave left for Bingo right on seven o'clock. Eyes down would be seven-thirty which gave him time to get his card and a good seat and have a beer before they started.

His brother showed at five past seven. Tonight, he was on foot. I was sitting across the street in my Monaro with the windows down. The sun was dropping in the west, and it was still about thirty-four degrees.

Dave's wife Felicity met Roger—yeah, that's right. Roger was rogering his brother's wife—on the front doorstep in a silken bathrobe. Immediately my Nikon went to work, its shutter doing overtime. For a moment I didn't think they were going to make it inside before the horizontal calisthenics started.

But they did, and it wasn't long before they had moved onto the dining room table going at it like rabbits.

I felt like a voyeur as I took more pictures of their cavorting. But I decided I had enough and now it was time to meet Nicole at the pub for steak and chips.

That was the idea. But as they say, sometimes the best laid plans go awry.

This time it was caused by Deadhead Dave arriving home. When I saw his old, battered SUV turn the corner at the end of the street my brain told me that something wasn't right.

I watched as he pulled into the drive and turned off the car. Meanwhile the pair inside were oblivious, still entangled and there was no way that Deadhead Dave could not see them.

Something was definitely wrong when he reached

into his rear seat and took out a rifle.

"Holy shit!" I exclaimed as I threw the Monaro's door open. My hand fumbled with my cell, and I was halfway across the dusty street when I found the right number.

"Mark—"

"Get over to Deadhead's, he's got a gun and he's going to kill someone."

Hanging up I broke into a run, hoping I would make it. And as I hit the steps the first shot rang out and I knew I was too late.

The paramedics loaded the body into the back of the ambulance. I looked at Nicole and said, "So much for dinner at the pub."

She nodded. "Doesn't seem right, does it?"

I glanced in the direction she was looking and said, "You're right, they're the ones who were screwing around and Deadhead is the one who dies. I hope that every time they close their eyes, they see him blowing his fucking brains out."

My voice was all but a snarl by the time I finished, and Nicole grabbed my hand. "Go home, Mark. I'll be there soon."

Jace appeared. "The rifle was registered to the deceased."

"Thanks, Jace."

He walked off and left us on our own. Nicole said, "I still have work to do. Will you be all right?"

"Yeah."

"Go home."

"All right."

"Love you."

"Love you, too."

CHAPTER TWO

If I thought the following day was going to be better, I was wrong. The sun was up early bringing its all-encompassing heat. A crow cawed loudly beside the bedroom window, and somehow a mosquito had gotten past the screens into our room and divebombed me all night.

I dragged my sorry ass out at ten past six. Nicole followed me about thirty minutes later. Like nothing was wrong. She took one look at me and said, "Eww, what happened to you?"

I opened my mouth to speak but instead, shook my head and replied, "Nothing."

Nicole scratched her shoulder. "I think a mosquito must have gotten in last night."

I rolled my eyes and reached for the coffee pot. She saw my movement and said, "I'll have one of those."

Two coffees later and Nicole was ready for work once more and I wasn't even dressed. "What are you going to do, today?"

"Go cooler hunting I guess."

As Nicole walked past, she kissed my shoulder. "With

everything that's happening, I don't know what time I'll be back."

Her cell rang and she answered. "What's up, Jace?"

She listened for a while and then spoke, then listened, then spoke some more. "Did you ring Rural Crimes?"

More listening. "Uh, huh. And you told them what we were in the middle of?"

More listening. Then, "Leave it with me."

She disconnected and stared straight at me. "I might have something to keep you busy for a while."

I looked at her suspiciously. "Like what?"

"I need you to go out to Joondalup Station and see Jack Mason. He's got a missing bull."

My eyebrows shot up. "A missing bull?"

"Yes. It's one of his prize studs."

"Isn't that a police matter?"

"Yes, but Rural Crimes don't want to come all the way out here until we've made sure that it hasn't wandered through a fence onto a neighbor's property. But after last night we still have—"

"All right, I'll go and have a look."

She gave me a brief kiss, took a drink from my tepid coffee and said, "You're the best. Love you, see you this evening. Maybe we can do that dinner thing."

"The one where I eat food off your body?" I asked her with more than a hint of sarcasm.

"Idiot."

"Love you, too."

"Oh, and take a rifle. The wild dogs out that way have been really bad lately."

I heard the door close and stared into my cup. Had I known then what kind of trouble a missing bull was going to cause, I'd have gone back to bed.

As the Monaro bottomed out on the rutted track which led to the Joondalup homestead for maybe the hundredth time, I knew I should have used some of the money that I'd earned from Marion Lawler to buy a damn 4X4. Each time it hit, the vehicle shuddered and sent a sharp jolt of pain up my spine.

Then to top it off, the Monaro's aircon packed it in and I was forced to drive with the window down so that the hot air blowing across the landscape could 'cool' me.

As I drove past a tall gum, I heard a crow making its horrible sound and for a moment I contemplated that it might be the same one from earlier in the day come back to haunt me.

The homestead itself was quite large and had been in the family for generations. It was a family run thing. Personally, I didn't know how they did it; after all, family and business were a bad mix.

I let the Monaro roll to a stop and killed the engine. The first thing to greet me—even before my cloud of dust could envelop me—were the station dogs. Maybe twenty of them. From somewhere nearby I heard a voice snarl, "Get out of it, ya bloody mongrels."

Then they just disappeared.

Climbing out, I saw a solidly built man wearing filthy jeans and a shirt with the sleeves torn out. He looked me up and down and said, "You lost?"

"Not if you're Jack Mason," I replied.

"Nope, I'm Tom Mason, his son."

Looking through the dirt and grime on his face I could see that he was indeed younger than he appeared. "Jack around?"

"Depends, what do you want?"

I opened my mouth to speak when a woman appeared and called out, "Who's that, Tom?"

"Just finding out," he called back.

The woman approached us. She was wearing jeans and a sleeveless T-shirt. From her Akubra hat, long black hair flowed down. "Looks kinda handsome," she said.

"Every new bloke looks handsome to you."

"Bet you he could plow a field."

"The only field you want him to plow is yours," Tom said dryly.

"Who are you, stud?"

"Mark Hayes," I replied hesitantly, thinking that if the woman were a tiger, she'd eat me for lunch.

"I'm Betty Mason. Heath and Paula's daughter. I'm twenty-two and single."

"Shit, Betty," Tom growled.

"What? I'm getting older every day. Girl needs to find herself a stud bull."

"That's why I'm here," I said to them. When I saw the look on Betty's face, I knew I should have chosen my words better.

When she smiled and took a step forward, Tom said, "Get lost, Betty. He's here to see Jack."

She pouted. "Bloody pity. Jack is over in the machinery shed."

I followed Tom over to the shed where we found Jack working. He was head down over a motor in a battered Land Cruiser. He looked up and stared at me. "Who the bloody hell are you?"

Got to love a country man. Straight to the point. No time to muck around. "I'm Mark Hayes. Sergeant Nicole Berger sent me out to see you."

He frowned. "What about?"

"A missing bull."

"You? Come all the way out here to find a missing bull? What a load of fucking shit."

He buried his head back under the hood of the Land Cruiser. I said, "Rural Crimes wanted her to check it out to see that your bull wasn't in somebody else's paddock. They didn't want to come up here for stuff all. She sent me out here to look around because she's up to her armpits in some guy that blew his brains out in his frigging kitchen last night. Now I can look around if you want, which I'm pretty good at, or I could jump in my car and piss off."

"What do you mean you're good at?"

"Part of my job is finding people that have gone missing. I figure a bull can't be that much harder."

His eyes narrowed. "What exactly do you do?"

"I'm a private investigator."

Recognition reached his face. "Now I know you. You're that bloke that shot all them people there a while back. Found the killer of all them girls that went missing."

"That's me." It was nothing to be proud of. There was one of those girls that I still felt guilty over.

"Do you reckon you can find it?"

"Can't hurt to have a look."

Jack Mason nodded. "Alright then. I'll get Tom to take you out to the paddock where he last was. Don't expect him to hang around, though. He's got work to do. You'll have to do everything yourself."

"Wouldn't have it any other way."

"And call me Jack."

"Mark."

With that, he went back to work on his motor. As though I wasn't even there.

I followed Tom back outside. He turned to me and said, "I'll just get the farm ute. Get in that thing you have there and follow me."

"I'll be right behind you."

The Monaro bounced around over the rough track as we drove out to the bull paddock. At one point we had to cross a dry wash, on which the Monaro bottomed out once again. Note to self. Buy 4X4.

We passed through two more gates, around behind some thick scrub, over a low rise, then around through another gateway into a much larger, open paddock. By this time, we were at least 2 kilometers from the main house.

Tom pulled the farm ute over and climbed out. "This is the paddock Barney was in."

"Barney?"

"Yeah, that's what we called him. Useless big lump he was. Good at impregnating cows though."

I looked around the paddock. All I could see was dry ground covered with brittle grass. To the west I saw a line of trees and a concrete water trough with a tank beside it. And to the north was another line of trees, although this one was further away. "What's up there?" I asked.

"It's a gravel road."

"Who uses it?" I asked.

"About four or five different station owners. It gives access to a lot of land."

"It also gives access to this one," I pointed out.

"I had a look over there. Nothing out of place."

"Before you go, I just need you to answer a couple more questions."

Tom looked at me, but then he nodded. "What do you want to know?"

"Was the bull always in this paddock?"

"No, not usually. We shifted him in here a week ago because there was more feed."

Once more, my eyes roamed over the paddock. I'd hate to see one without any feed. Yet this was the paddock that they'd chosen to put a one-ton bull in. "So where was he normally?"

"Three kilometers east."

"Any access from the roads over there?" I asked.

"No. You have to drive through about six paddocks to get to it."

"One more before you go. Whose idea was it to shift him?"

"Does it matter?" Tom asked defensively.

"Just trying to get a picture of everything."

"You sound like a cop."

I nodded. "Used to be one."

"No shit?"

"Now I'm what they call a rent-a-cop. Probably not even that. A rental investigator."

Tom chuckled.

"So whose idea was it to shift him?"

"It was mine."

"Thanks. You can go back now if you want. I'll have a look around."

"Just ask if you want anything else."

"I almost forgot. How much was Barney worth?"

"As a bull, bugger all. As a breeder, he was worth a bloody fortune."

"Thanks, Tom."

He took off in the ute, leaving me alone with a pall of dust, the heat, and the flies. I stood for a moment in the deafening silence and listened. It was broken by a Sulphur Crested Cockatoo screeching in a nearby tree. Then a flock of galahs joined in with their own fruity sound.

I opened the back door on the Monaro and took out a bolt-action Weatherby .223 rifle with a scope on top. I slipped home the five-round magazine and didn't worry about taking extra ammo. The last thing I grabbed was a bottle of water. Get caught or stuck out here without one and things can turn out really bad.

Using all of my detecting skills I walked north. I mean if you want to get a bull out of his paddock the easiest way is by road. Even though Tom had said it was checked, I wanted to look for myself.

It took me a while to reach the fence line, but once I did, I headed to my left and followed it along the trees. With each step, dust rose from beneath the heels of my shoes. The fence was tight. Each strand stretched, so when you grabbed it, it just twanged back into place.

I kept my eyes on the ground, looking, watching. A four-wheel drive drove past as I continued my search, a rooster tail of dust following it along the road hanging in the air like a giant curtain.

I felt the breeze pick up, with it, a subtle sense of cooler air. I looked out to the west and saw a buildup of darkening clouds. A storm was coming, and when it broke, it would wash away any trace of what had happened to the bull.

I almost missed it. It was that faint on the hard packed earth that the paw print almost didn't stand out against its dusty background. A dog had been here. It could, however, be that of a wild dog. I didn't know.

Leaning over the fence, my eyes ran along the other side where the grass, although dry and dead looking, was substantially longer.

Further along I found a gap in the tree line. It wasn't much but I paid closer attention to it because of what was there. Hair on a broken branch of one of the trees. Not a lot and it was on my side of the fence. Which was quite normal.

My immediate instinct, however, was to look down. I saw nothing. No dog prints, no bull marks, and the earth was bare except for the dust. Dust that was showing my boot imprints as clear as the end of my nose. Admittedly the hair could have been old, but I doubted it.

I walked out further from the fence line, clear of the trees. My eyes darting left and right as they swept the area for any signs which might help with my investigation. Then I saw what I was looking for.

I may not be a bushy, or a country person, but I considered myself to be a damned good investigator. Back to what I found. Boot marks and pawprints. Two, maybe three people and one dog.

Moving further back from the fence and trees my search was suddenly interrupted by the low rumble of thunder in the distance. I lifted my head and glanced to the west. The iron-gray clouds had grown curtains beneath from which voluminous amounts of water were dropping.

Now I needed to work fast.

I looked back down at the ground. Amongst the sparse tufts of grass, I saw marks the bull had left behind. Also, there were boot marks and pawprints. Looking up I saw that they were all headed to where I had just come from.

I took some pictures with my phone before hurrying forward to the fence again. I looked at it closely, moving about twenty meters in either direction until I found it. The fence had been cut and expertly rejoined. Away from where I'd found the hair.

Thoughts filled my mind for a moment and then I tried the next two posts in line. Neither was as solid as they should have been. Whoever had taken the bull, had also removed the posts then put them back.

After taking pictures, I climbed the fence and walked out onto the road. While the rain drew closer, I walked each side of the gravel road both ways for fifty meters. There would be no way whoever stole the bull would risk taking it further. I was right. They'd used a truck with a ramp. I could see the marks on the road. The bull had walked right up on it.

Once more I took pictures, this time of the marks as well as tire imprints. Not before time because I felt the first drop of rain fall from the rapidly graying clouds helped along by a sharp gust of wind and the crash of thunder signaling the storm's arrival.

After clambering over the fence, I started back to where the Monaro was parked. By the time I reached it, the rain was coming down hard and I was soaked through.

The Monaro was coated with mud when I finally reached the yard at the homestead. Rain and thick dust combine quickly to become a sticky situation in the outback. I turned the beast off and climbed out into the deluge. When I entered the machinery shed, I found Jack, Tom, and Betty Mason all standing around the Land Cruiser that Jack had been working on earlier.

They stared at me, Betty possibly a little more eagerly than the rest. I think it was something to do with the way my shirt clung to me now that it was wet. I'm not one to brag, but even with my substantial diet I don't cut a bad figure.

"Would you look at what the cat dragged in," Mason growled.

"I am," said Betty with an appreciative smile.

"Well, city boy, what have you got?"

"Most likely nothing," Tom said.

"Your bull was stolen—"

"I already frigging know that," he snapped, cutting me off.

"Your bull was stolen by three people and a dog."

His glare demanded that I tell him more.

"They cut your fence and removed a couple of posts to throw everything off. They then loaded the bull onto a truck in the middle of the road and drove off."

"That fucking mongrel, Morrison," Mason swore. "I bet it was that bastard."

"Who is Morrison?"

"He's a neighbor lives down that road."

"What is his first name?" I asked.

"Vince. He's a pommy bastard from England."

Tom gave me a funny look. "How did you work all this out when I didn't even find a thing?"

I stared at him. "Maybe because you weren't looking for what I was."

He kicked the floor and said nothing.

I said to Jack Mason, "I need the names of your other neighbors. Maybe they saw something down there."

"Aren't you meant to be handing this off to Rural Crimes?"

I nodded. "That's the plan, but someone has to ask the questions before they get here. Could be a couple of days."

"How about we say bugger them and you just do it?"

"Are you sure that's the way you want to go?"

"How much is it going to cost me?"

"Five-hundred a day."

"Dad—" Tom started.

"Shut up."

"We can't afford it," Tom protested.

"I told you to shut up. This doesn't concern you, boy. This is my bull."

"I tell you what. I'll have a look around for the first few days, and if I don't think I can find your bull I won't charge you anything. If I do, you pay me everything. How about that?"

Mason's face turned hard. "Don't need charity. Especially someone from the city like you."

I shrugged. "Suit yourself."

Turning away, I started to walk off. "Where the bloody hell are you going?" Mason called after me.

"Home. I'm wet, I'm tired, and I've got a fucking mosquito to find."

CHAPTER THREE

After a shower, I dried off and put on fresh clothes. I looked at the time. It was 3:30 in the afternoon. I still had at least an hour and a half to kill before Nicole was finished, so I decided to put that time to good use and see a man who might be able to help me track down what type of truck I was looking for.

Outside, the rain had stopped, and steam rose from the street. The smell of damp earth filled the air, made so by the recent precipitation. Large puddles had formed as well, a sign of the intensity of what had come down. I wondered if it had fallen in the right place for runoff to start filling Friar's Lake. After all, it was getting close to that time of the year.

That thought led to others. The girls they'd found there, of Tash, of Helen. It had been almost twelve months and there was still no word. The time with Nicole had been good though. I hardly spoke to Tia now. Something I was sure she was grateful for.

I turned the corner and ahead I saw my destination. The secondhand car yard run by Cyril, the man who'd sold me the Monaro.

As I walked into the car yard my boots crunched on the gravel. It worked the same way a bell on a store door lets an owner know someone is coming. He came out of his office, the smile on his face quickly disappearing when he saw who it was. "It's you."

As usual his beard was bushy, and his suit crumpled.

"Is that any way to greet a potential customer?" I asked him.

"Are you?"

"Am I what?"

"A potential customer?"

"Ah, no." My thoughts strayed to needing to purchase a four-wheel drive.

"Then piss off."

"Come on, Cyril—"

"No, Mark. The last time I got involved with you, people wound up dead."

"In all fairness, mate, most of them were already dead."

"What do you want?"

"I believe you're a man of knowledge," I replied with a broad grin.

Cyril shook his head. "Turn it up. Don't you know that you can't bullshit a bullshitter?"

I took my phone out of my pocket and brought up a picture. "I took a photo of some tire marks. I wanted you to look at them."

Cyril took the phone when I held it out for him. He looked at it, frowned, and said, "Bridgestone M766 drive tire."

"Just like that?"

He nodded. "Just like that."

"How do you know shit just like that?" I asked him, astounded by his knowledge.

"I just do. It's nothing special."

Bullshit it wasn't. I was lucky to remember what I did a few days ago. That reminded me. I took out a pen and paper and wrote down what he'd told me. "Bridgestone, you say?"

He handed me back my phone. "Sure. What are you up to, anyway?"

"Looking for a missing bull."

Cyril raised his eyebrows. "Really? I would have thought there wouldn't be enough excitement in something like that for you."

I knew what he was getting at. I grinned at him. "I'm not shooting people this week."

"That's a relief. Say, did they find that girl that was taken when that big shootout happened?"

He was talking about Helen Miller.

"No, not yet."

Cyril stared at me. He could tell it bothered me so changed the subject. "Whose bull is missing?"

"Jack Mason, Joondalup Station."

"That bastard," Cyril growled.

"Don't like him?" I asked.

"Prick owes me money," Cyril said. "Don't think I should hold my breath about getting it, either."

"Why do you say that?"

"He's up to his balls in debt. Got me stuffed how he's still out there."

Interesting. I knew from my visit that things out there might have been tight, but the way Cyril was talking, they might be a fair bit worse. "I kind of got that feeling but I didn't think things were that bad."

"I think you'll find that they are."

I nodded. "What's the go out there anyway? Family run affairs usually don't work out that well."

"Jack and Heath Mason were left the station when

their parents died. It was an equal split. Dot is Jack's wife and Tom is his son."

I nodded. "I met Jack and Tom while I was out there."

"Heath the brother is married to Paula. She's a city girl. Came up from Adelaide. Don't know why, she's still as city as they come."

"Nope, still to meet them."

"You're not missing anything."

"Met the daughter though. Actually, she almost ate me on the spot."

Cyril chuckled. "She's a real man-eater that one. Never used to be. I remember when she was a kid she was as quiet as a mouse. Went away to school and once she was done, she came back. Gone was the innocent kid."

"What's Tom like?"

The used car salesman shrugged. "Hard worker. Bled sweat and tears into that place."

"His old man seems to give him a hard time," I pointed out.

"You would, too, if he weren't your son."

I gave him a quizzical look. "Tom isn't Jack's?"

"So the story goes."

"Is that just bush telegraph or truth?" I asked.

"It's not confirmed. Word was that Dot got pregnant with Tom while Jack was up north droving for a couple of months."

"So it's just a rumor," I said.

"Make of it what you will." Cyril shrugged and turned to walk away.

I was about to do the same when I stopped. "Who in town sells the truck tires, Cyril?"

He stopped walking and turned side on, holding out his right hand, palm face upward. With a frown I asked, "What?"

"Information don't come free, you know."

After all the time I'd just spent asking him questions, he picked now to ask for payment. I sighed. "How much?"

"Hundred."

"You're kidding."

"Man's time is worth something," he shot back at me.

I muttered a curse and took out my wallet. Passing a couple of fifties over, I said, "You're a bloody thief."

He just grinned and put the money in his pocket.

"Well, are you going to say who it is?"

His grin got broader. "Me."

"Christ, Cyril."

He chuckled.

"Can you tell me who bought the tires?" I asked.

"I'll need a day or so to go through my books but off the top of my head there are only a few."

"How can you be so sure?"

"It's like the tire marks, it's just there."

I nodded. "Give me a call when you're done, please."

"Sure. Just one problem."

"What's that?"

"I don't have your number."

I gave him the number and left. Retracing my footsteps until I reached the main street, I stopped at the local men's apparel store. Inside was dim, almost dingy, lined with dark wood, which was still there, I figured, from when it opened back in the early nineteen-twenties. It held a certain smell about it, too. The one made up of dust, floor polish, and years of clothes, shoes, and anything else that had once graced it.

A young woman wearing black pants and a white

blouse sought me out across the room. She was currently serving an older gentleman. "I'll be right with you, sir."

"No problem, take your time."

She smiled at me and went back to wrapping the man's purchase in a sheet of brown paper. Who uses brown paper in this day and age?

I, meanwhile, went to the shoe section. I looked at several rows of them in front of me. Dress shoes, runners, work boots, casual slip-ons. They were all there, but it was the work boots that interested me.

It was the usual setup. The lids were off so the customer could get access to try on what was on offer. I started picking through the work boots, checking out their soles.

"Can I help you, sir?"

I turned and saw the young woman standing there smiling at me with unusually white teeth. "Ah, yes," I replied, reaching into my pocket for my phone. I took it out and showed her the boot tread pattern I was looking for. "I was hoping you could tell me what brand these are?"

She took a quick look and said, "Desert Tracks."

I shook my head. "No, it was taken in a paddock."

She grinned at me, her teeth trying once more to burn my retinas. "No, silly. That's the brand. They're made right here in New South Wales."

Shit. "I knew that," I replied, trying to rescue my pride.

"Right."

She moved to her left a touch and reached out with her left hand. I noted on the inside of her forearm was a small tattoo of some Asian symbol. "Been to China?" I asked.

"Pardon?" She gave me a puzzled look.

"The tattoo."

"Charlie's Ink Parlor here in town."

This was going well.

"Here they are."

She took a boot from an open box. The footwear was deep brown in color with laces instead of pull tabs. She passed it to me, and I turned it over. The tread pattern was a match. "I suppose there are a lot of people in town who buy these?"

"Not really."

"Could you get me a list?"

Her expression took on an apprehensive look. "I—I don't think I should. Privacy and all that. I could get into trouble."

I nodded. I wasn't going to push it. Besides, I could get them another way. "That's fine—"

"Mary."

"That's fine, Mary. Thank you for your help."

I turned to leave but stopped. "The boots, Mary. Are they a good brand?"

"My boyfriend swears by them."

"Really?" I gave her my best smile. "Who's the lucky guy?"

She blushed for a moment and said, "Jim Kelly. He's a plumber here in town."

Later that evening while I ate heartily at the Friar's Lake pub, Nicole opened the can of worms that I knew was bubbling just below the surface. "Are you going to tell me about the missing bull or not?"

I could see she wasn't too happy about having to ask, but in truth I was still trying to put some of the pieces together in my mind. Her hair was down, and she wore a short blue dress which looked amazing on her. "You look lovely this evening."

"Wow, you noticed."

"Sorry."

There was a moment of silence. "Well?"

"Oh, Jack Mason has hired me to find out what happened to his bull," I told her.

"What about Rural Crimes?"

"I don't know. Not my department. Maybe he doesn't want them involved."

"Was the bull stolen?" Nicole asked as she put the last of her battered fish into her mouth.

I nodded. "Most definitely. The fence was cut, and the animal was loaded onto the back of a truck."

"You told him this?"

"Yes."

"Maybe I'll go and have a word with him tomorrow," Nicole said. "What else did you find out?"

"I'm still running down a few things," I replied. "Speaking of which—"

"No." Her tone left little room for maneuver.

"Nicole—"

"No, Mark."

"Just one little favor?"

She sighed indignantly. "Is this what Tia went through all the time?"

"Not at first."

"What do you want?"

I told her about the footwear.

"I'll have a talk to her."

"Thank you."

"What else have you discovered?"

"Not much. I have a few ideas, but nothing proven as yet."

Suddenly our conversation was interrupted by shouting from the main bar. I looked at Nicole and said,

"What is it with this frigging place?"

She stood up and I followed her lead. We walked out into the bar and found two women going at it, hammer and tongs. One had a handful of hair while the other was trying to scratch her opponent's eyes out with clawed fingers. Without thinking, we moved through the cheering crowd and proceeded to separate the two combatants.

As they were prised apart, I heard the one I held yell out, "Let go of my tit, you pervert prick!"

Suddenly I realized she was right; my hand was full of—then something else hit me like a bullet between my eyes. The person I had hold of was Betty Mason.

Like I'd just dipped my hands in lava, I released her. She broke away and whirled, hand raised, ready to punch me in the mouth. Then she, too, saw who it was. "Oh. It's you."

"Yeah, sorry."

"Be right back."

She whirled like a dust devil and launched herself towards her opponent who was currently struggling to free herself from Nicole's grasp.

I have to say, I've not seen a right hook to this day that could match the one that screamed out of nowhere and smashed into the other girl's chin. Now this lass was by no means small. On a scale from one to ten, I would say huge. Not fat, just solid, all muscle. Yet when that bunched fist connected, it made almost every one of the male onlookers cringe as the eyes rolled back into her head and she started to sag towards the stained, carpeted floor.

Then, as casually as you like, Betty turned back to face me and said, "Now, where were we?"

I smiled at her. "I think you might be going to jail."

Betty winked at me as Jace led her out the back to the cells. Nicole shook her head and asked me, "What is it with you and her? Something you want to tell me?"

"Yes, I feel like a lump of meat that a tiger wants to devour."

Nicole chuckled. "My guess is that she has you lined up for a three-course meal, sunshine."

"Can we go home?"

"Soon. There are a couple of things I need to take care of."

"At least we got to finish our meal."

"Don't forget we didn't get dessert."

I gave her a sly grin. "I figure you've got that covered."

While Nicole finished what she had to do, I went over to the wall of the forgotten where several posters hung for missing persons. Roughly 30,000 people go missing each year; of those over half are kids aged between 11 and 17 years.

"Trouble just seems to follow you, doesn't it?" Jace said to me after he'd locked Betty Mason up for the night.

"I guess I'm just lucky," I replied. "Tell me something, Jace. You've been here for a while. I think Nicole said you were born here, yes?"

"That's right."

"You ever heard the rumor that Tom Mason isn't Jack's son?"

He nodded. "Yep, heard it before."

"How do they get on?"

"All right, I guess. Bit hard on him at times."

"Do you figure that Tom'll get his share when the time comes?" I asked.

Jace nodded. "I guess so. There's only him and Betty."

"What does Betty think of it?"

"How do you mean?"

I said, "Tom's not part of the family but he's still getting his share."

Jace shrugged. "It's not like he hasn't earned it. He's worked hard. They all seem to get on."

"All?"

"You know, him, Betty. They have the same circle of friends."

"What friends?"

"Is this still about the bull?"

"Could be. Is Jim Kelly part of that circle?" I asked.

"Sure."

"Who else?"

"Bluey Timms, Gerald Long, Nellie Brown, and Jimmy Morrison."

"Jimmy Morrison? Is he the neighbor's son?"

"That's right."

"I didn't think they got on," I said.

"The old ones don't," Jace said. "The younger ones are different."

"Thanks for that."

"Anytime."

I thought for a moment. "One more thing. Do you know anything about them having money problems?"

Jace grunted. "They're land and stock owners. Who isn't having cash flow troubles?"

"Yes, you're right. Thanks."

"If he's trying to con you into doing something, Jace, don't let him. That's an order."

I turned and gave Nicole a sarcastic smile. "You have absolutely no faith in your fellow human being."

"And every faith in what you're up to being no good. Come on, we're going home. You good, Jace?"

"I'll be fine, boss. Murph comes on soon."

Murph was Constable Jessie Murphy, a new constable sent out to the ass end of hell as her first posting. In the review after everything went down the year before, New South Wales Police Force decided that because of the expanse of the area the district covered, an extra constable to the region was warranted. That meant four coppers instead of three. Murphy being one, and another being Byron Vince. I guess I didn't mention that when I started.

This meant that Jace had been promoted to senior constable.

The door crashed open and a young woman of about twenty stumbled in. She had blonde hair tied up in a bun and pretty features even if they were currently a deep shade of red. "Shit! Fu—oh, hi." She tried to gather herself upon seeing us all staring in her direction.

"Trouble with the step again, Constable?" Nicole asked.

"Yes, Sarge, sorry."

"Maybe one day you'll learn to pick your feet up."

"I'll try to remember that one."

Murph glanced at me, and I gave her a wink. "Don't worry, Murph, her bite is much worse than her bark."

She looked even more confused now.

"What was that?" Nicole asked me incredulously. "You're a dick, Hayes."

"Yes, but I'm your—"

"Do not finish that sentence," she said and started pushing me towards the door. "Goodnight, everyone. I'll see you in the morning."

CHAPTER FOUR

I was up early the next morning. Too much running around in my head so I went for a jog to process it. Yes, that's right, a jog. A gut busting, sweat draining, calf tearing, concrete pounding run. It reminded me of my academy days.

And when it was complete, I stopped, turned, and looked back the fifty meters to the driveway I'd just left. One day my metabolism would catch up to me, but until now, the odd healthy meal kept it at bay.

"You don't look so good, Mark," a voice said from behind me.

I turned and saw Pru Jacobs with a worried expression on her face. I gave her a pained smile and said, "Rolled my ankle."

"Oh, do you need some help?"

"No, no, I should be fine."

"Maybe you should stick to walking," she said with a glimmer in her eye. "Less dangerous at your age."

"I'll do that."

"Anything about my cooler?"

"Not yet, but I'm working on it. I do have a question, though. Your plumber, do you use him all the time?"

"No, it was just that my regular man was busy. Jim Kelly is a good boy. I know his mother."

I nodded. "Thank you."

After she was gone, I took her advice and started walking, letting the processor in my head do its thing. But before it could get wound up, my cell rang.

"Hayes."

"Didn't wake you up, did I?" Cyril asked.

"Not this day," I replied.

"I have a few names for you if you want to drop by."

Looking at my watch, I said, "Be there at nine."

The call disconnected and I turned around and walked back to Nicole's place.

She was eating a bowl of cereal when I walked in. "That was quick," she said with a wry smile and a dribble of milk on her chin. "Forget something? Like how fit you are?"

I mumbled a few words under my breath about wearing a bib and learning to eat properly. She just smiled and held her bowl forward. "Want some?"

"If I wanted some, I'd lick your face."

"What? Oh." She wiped her chin. "What are you doing today?"

"I have a couple of things to follow up on. What about you?"

"This and that."

"Fair enough."

"There is one thing."

I looked at her and there was a funny expression on her face. "What might that be?"

"I think I might be pregnant."

A broad grin split my lips. "Yeah, good one."

I stared at her waiting for her to crack and a smile to

appear on her pretty face. But there wasn't a smile, not even a hint of a grin. There was, however, a look of worry. "Oh, shit, you're serious."

"Not the kind of reaction I was hoping for," she said to me and opened her mouth to speak but instead, stifled a sob and hurried off to her bedroom.

"Nicole, wait."

"Just fuck off."

Her words were savage and cut deeper than I expected. How on earth did she expect me to react? She drops a bomb on me and expects me not to be shocked by it all. Hell, we weren't that far along in our relationship. Sure, I loved her, but we'd never discussed marriage let alone having kids. At least I didn't ask her if it was mine.

I walked down the hallway to the bedroom door. It was locked. "Nic, open the door."

"Go away, Mark."

I could hear her crying. "Can we talk about this?"

"No, I don't want to talk to you."

"Nic—"

"Go away!"

"Are you sure about this?" I had to ask, right?

For a moment there was silence and then the door unlocked. It swung back suddenly and then I was hit in the chest with something which fell to the floor at my feet. I bent down and picked the item up. It was a pregnancy test.

And yes, it was positive.

I left the house after placing the test on the counter in the kitchen. It was too early to go and see Cyril, so I just walked as I processed what had just unfolded. I was full of mixed emotions. But then one kept rising to the surface. Fear. The thought of being a father scared the shit out of me. I needed to tell Nicole just so she understood.

The house was empty when I got back. Nicole had

already gone to work. The pregnancy test was still on the counter; she had left a note saying she had an appointment with her GP and that if I felt like it, I could attend with her at one-thirty.

Of course, I was going to go. Nothing would keep me away.

"What do you have for me, Cyril?" I asked as I walked into his office.

"Three names."

"Three?"

"Yes, surprisingly. I thought I'd sold more tires than that but apparently, I hadn't." He stared at me. "Are you all right? You don't look so good."

I'm fine. About to be the father of a screaming turd production line, but hey, it's all good. Did I really feel like that, or was it shock? "I'm good. Names."

"Vince Morrison, Lionel White, Harry Poole."

"I know where Morrison lives, what about White and Poole?"

"White lives out at Iron Pot Creek," Cyril replied.

"Where's that?"

"About twenty kilometers the other side of Hampton."

"Too far. What about Poole?"

"Barrow Road. About four kilometers south of town."

"Thanks, Cyril."

I left the car yard and headed back towards the main street. I mulled the news over in my head. Vince Morrison? Maybe too obvious. Poole? No link yet but it didn't mean there wasn't.

Suddenly I heard the squeal of tires and realized I was halfway across the street with a blue car coming for me at speed. I threw myself sideways, feeling the bite of bitumen into my exposed skin. The car hurtled past, barely missing me.

It disappeared as it turned left about a hundred meters further along before I could get a look at the number plate.

"Mark, are you alright?"

I looked up from where I sat in the middle of the main street and saw Yolanda Reed from the paper shop. "I'm still breathing."

"What a maniac," she said as I picked myself up. "Typical out-of-towner."

I glanced back at the empty street and then nodded. "Yeah, crazy."

"Oh, you're bleeding," Yolanda gasped.

I looked down at my forearm. "It's nothing. Just a bit of skin."

"Come over to—"

"Help me! Somebody, please help me!" My head snapped around and I saw Mary from the men's apparel store waving at us. "Help, I can't wake him up."

"You'd better call for ambulance and police, Yolanda," I snapped as I started running towards the distressed young woman.

As I reached her, Mary said, "Hurry, there's blood everywhere. I'm so scared."

"Show me where he is."

Jim Kelly lay unconscious in a bloody heap. Unresponsive. I checked his pulse and airway just to make sure all was good. I looked up at Mary and asked, "What happened?"

"I—I don't know, I just found him this way."

Already the sirens could be heard. Small town, not far for them to drive. Yolanda appeared. "They're on their way."

"Thank you. Could you take Mary and..."

She stared at me. "Of course."

"I should stay with him," Mary said.

"No," Yolanda said softly. "You come with me, dear. We'll just be in the way."

Minutes later the ambos and the police arrived. The paramedics stabilized Jim while the police asked questions.

By police I mean Nicole and Jessie Murphy. Jessie asked the questions while Nicole just glared at me. I decided to wait for an opening before I tried to talk to her.

"Mark, do you have a moment?"

I turned to face Murphy. "Sure?"

"Can I ask you how you became involved in this?"

"I was just walking past, and Mary came out all panicked. She was saying that she couldn't wake him."

She pointed at my right hand. "Bit of skin off your knuckles there. How did you get that?"

"By throwing myself on the road to avoid getting run over," I replied. "Yolanda saw it happen. Don't worry, Constable, it wasn't me that beat the crap out of him."

"I have to ask."

I nodded. "Sorry. Of course, you do."

"This car, do you think it could be tied up with this?"

Raising my eyebrows, I nodded. "Possible, I guess. Now that I have a chance to think about it, the driver was reasonably erratic. So could be."

She took her pad and pencil making notes as I talked. "Make? Color?"

"Blue car, can't tell you the make."

"Number plate?"

"Sorry."

"Never mind. It's a start. Color is better than nothing."

"Maybe Yolanda will have better recall."

"Maybe."

Murphy walked over to Nicole. They talked for a moment before the constable moved on to Yolanda. Nicole on the other hand came over to me. "Are you alright?"

"I'm fine." I held up my hand. "Bit of bark off. Nothing much."

She winced, her expression genuine. She opened her mouth to speak but I cut her off. "I'm sorry, Nic. I could have handled this morning better."

She glanced around to make sure no one was listening, but the ambos were busy as was Murphy still talking to Yolanda. "Not here, Mark."

"Fine, when?"

"Are you coming to the appointment?"

"Of course, I am." My voice came out curt, indignant. "Sorry. Yes, I'll be there."

"We'll talk then."

She started to turn away, but I grabbed her arm. "Nic, I love you."

She turned her head, and I could see the tears in her eyes. "I love you, too, Mark."

That was where we left it. We'd talk later. I looked at my watch. I had time.

Mary was standing next to the ambulance as they loaded Jim Kelly into it. I walked over to her. "How is he?"

"They don't know. He may have to go to Dubbo. Depends on what the doctors say. If he needs scans he'll just go to Griffith."

"Did you see the car that left here, Mary?" I asked.

She shook her head. "No."

"Hear it?"

She frowned. She started shaking her head but as it

began moving it bobbed up and down. "Yes, I think so. Could whoever was in it be responsible?"

"I don't know. I told the constable so maybe she might be able to come up with something."

"We're going. Miss, did you want to come with us?"

Mary turned to the ambo. "Yes, please."

"Just hop in up front."

I watched the ambulance go and left the police to conduct the rest of their investigation. Maybe I would just go back to Nic's and contemplate fatherhood. Then I saw my arch nemesis watching from across the street.

I walked over to him. "Hey, Tommy, how's it going? No school?"

He looked up at me with suspicion in his quickly narrowing brown eyes. "What do you want?"

"Been here long?"

"Long enough."

"Do you like cars, Tommy?"

"Maybe."

"I do. I've got a Monaro, goes like a shower of sh—" I paused. "It just goes well."

"Piece of junk. You need a Fairlane Five Hundred."

I nodded. "Not like that blue car earlier, huh? The Mazda that almost ran me over."

"Wasn't a Mazda, it was—" He stopped.

"It was what?"

"Never saw it."

"You sure?"

"You saying I'm a liar?" he asked indignantly.

I reached into my pocket and found my wallet. I opened it up and took out a tenner. I held it out. Tommy looked at me and then crept his hand forward.

"Car, Tommy?"

"BMW Series 4 Coupe."

"You sure?"

"Shit, I'm sure."

I handed the money over and said, "Don't spend it all at once."

He snatched it from my hand and ran off. The last I saw of him he was headed for the newspaper shop. Possibly going to buy a car magazine. *Or steal it,* the cynical side of me thought.

"You hassling the youth of Friar's Lake again?"

It was Nic which surprised me. "Just investigating."

"Get any answers?"

"Blue BMW Series 4 Coupe."

"Wow."

"The kid knows his cars."

She stood in silence. I could sense that she wanted to say more but all that happened was things got awkward. "I'll see you at one-thirty."

Nic's head bobbed. "Yes, one-thirty. Lake Street Clinic."

"Got it."

What to do until then? I went back to see Cyril.

"You forget something?" he asked, sarcasm lacing his voice.

"Blue BMW Series 4 Coupe."

"What about it?"

"Anyone in town got one?"

The derisive snort exploded from his lips. "This is Friar's Lake, Hayes. Something like that is way too fancy for here."

"Yeah, I guess so."

"Why are you asking?"

"If you hear about one, can you let me know?"

He nodded. "Sure."

"Thanks."

I sat next to Nicole and looked around the waiting room at all the eyes staring back at me. Or was it the uniformed cop beside me? Whoever it was, it felt like being in an enclosure at the zoo, with crowds gawking at me.

Nic tapped my leg. I glanced at her. "What's wrong?" she whispered out of the side of her mouth.

"People are staring."

"No, they're not."

"The hell—yes they are," I whispered.

A slight smile touched her lips. The first I'd seen since the blowup that morning. She reached out and squeezed my hand.

A couple of minutes later one of the office ladies said, "Sergeant Berger, the doctor will see you now."

She may as well have screamed it from the rooftops. Hey, the sarge is here, she's up the duff. Christ.

We stood together and I began to follow Nicole. I hesitated momentarily, thinking I'd heard a voice I knew. I turned but I couldn't see anyone familiar. So I continued along a narrow hallway and then to the right. We stopped outside a door with a sign advising us that it was the office of a Doctor Harrison. Nicole opened it and we went in.

The doctor was a younger woman, possibly not long in the job and forced to practice out in the sticks where the need was high. She smiled warmly. "Hello, Nicole."

"Hello, Amy."

Amy, was it?

"I see you have company."

"Yes, my partner, Mark."

She nodded in my direction. "Mark. Pleased to meet you."

"Doc."

"Now, Nicole, what can I do for you?"

"I think I might be pregnant."

"You've done a test?" Harrison asked.

"Yes, it was positive."

The doctor nodded. "All right then, I'll do a few tests of my own to confirm it. How do you feel?"

"Scared shitless."

Both women looked at me. Had I said that out loud? Nicole's glare told me I had. "Fuck."

We went home after the meeting with the doctor. Nicole was quiet, as was I, my performance hanging like a dark cloud over us both. I'd tried to salvage something from the wreck, but it was a losing battle so on the advice of the doctor, I remained silent.

"Do you want me to have the baby?" Nic asked out of the blue.

I turned to her and stared at her red-rimmed eyes. "What do you want to do?"

"That's not what I asked you, Mark."

Was this a trap? One of those questions that there was no correct answer to and that I couldn't get right no matter how I answered it. "Nic, I'm not the one who has to put their career on hold for a time and carry the baby. Hell, we're not even married."

"Answer the question, damn you. I need to know where you stand in all of this. Are you in or out?"

I opened my mouth to speak when the cell began ringing in my pocket. I took it out and then looked at Nicole and shrugged. "I have to take this."

She glared at me as though I'd planned it. "Hello?"

"Mark? It's Pru Jacobs."

"What can I do for you, Pru?"

"You won't believe this, but my cooler has reappeared."

Thank God. "Wonderful news."

"Maybe. But it has something in it."

"What do you mean, something?"

She sounded confused. "I'm not sure. Maybe you could come and have a look?"

"All right, give me about twenty minutes."

"Thank you, goodbye."

She disconnected the call, and I looked across the counter to where Nic was seated at the kitchen table. "Yes," I said.

She looked at me, confused. "What?"

"You asked if I wanted to have this baby with you, did you not?"

She nodded. "Yes."

"Nic, I'm not going to lie, it scares the hell out of me. Especially with the line of work we're both in."

"We could work something out."

That right there was favorable. It proved to me she wanted to keep the baby. Was going to keep the baby whether I was in or out. And surprisingly, I was in. "Yes, Nic. Yes, I'm in all the way."

She came off the seat and around the end of the counter as though she was flying above the floor. She cannoned into me, almost knocking me over, joy exploding from her.

After a couple of minutes kissing, babbling, going over the top with joy, I said, "I have to go and see Pru Jacobs. Her cooler has resurfaced."

"I'll come with you."

"Are you sure?" I asked her.

"Sure. You can fill me in on what you have."

"All right, but I must warn you, it's boring shit."

"I can't imagine that it is at all."

CHAPTER FIVE

Before long we were in Nicole's work vehicle with her driving and me telling her where I was at. It was good; she was the sounding board I needed, and being a copper, she had a different perspective on things.

"I told you about the bull, right?"

"Yes."

"It was loaded onto a truck. I went to see Cyril about tires, and he came up with some names. Mason blames his neighbor which happens to be one of the names Cyril came up with."

"Have you been to see him?"

I stared at her.

"No, of course you haven't."

"I'll go and see him tomorrow."

"Any theories yet?" Nicole asked.

"Why would I have a theory?"

"I don't know. You Jim Rockford types *always* have a theory." She was playing with me.

"How much would a bull like that be worth?" I asked.

"Why?"

"Mason is having money problems."

"You think he's stolen his own bull for insurance? Why not just sell it? It doesn't make sense."

"What if he claimed the insurance and then tried to pass it off as another?"

"Easily identified, brands and such."

"Yeah, I suppose." Another question came into my head. "Did you manage to get a list of people with those boots I told you about?"

"Sorry, no."

"Never mind."

We pulled up in the driveway and climbed out of Nicole's vehicle. Pru met us before we got to the door. "You brought backup, Mark? Hardly a dangerous situation."

"The sergeant was at a loose end, so she came to make sure I didn't take advantage of you."

Pru smiled. "Hello, Sergeant."

"Hello, Mrs. Jacobs."

"Please, I've told you before to call me Pru. You've been here too many years now."

"Then you have to call me Nicole and not Sergeant."

"I will."

"Now you ladies are reacquainted and all, how about we go and check out the missing cooler?" I suggested.

As we walked along the side of her home, Pru Jacobs said, "It's all really strange. It was there, then gone, and now it's back."

"You said it had something in it."

"Yes, you'll have to look at it. I've no idea what they are."

When we reached the gate to the back yard, Pru reached into her pocket and pulled out a key, placing it into the padlock and opening it. We went around the back, and right next to the air conditioning unit was the cooler. I took out the picture I had been given the day before and compared them. I looked at Nicole and winked. "Yes, that is the cooler in question."

I leaned down and removed the lid expecting to see some beers or— "Nope, not that."

"See what I mean?"

My head crooked to one side, and I said, "What the hell are they?"

Whatever they were, they were thin, around ten centimeters in length, and done up in bundles and floating in water.

"Semen straws," Nicole said from where she was looking over my shoulder.

"I beg your pardon?"

"Semen straws. They're what they put semen in when they milk bulls or stallions."

"What about humans?" I couldn't help myself and a sharp elbow to the ribs was what I earned.

"Oh dear," Pru gasped. "Is all that liquid in there semen?"

I turned away as I tried to mask the smirk that immediately came to my lips. My head was full to bursting with so many retorts that were backed up in my throat. But to expel them ran the risk of at least one or two bullets from Nicole's sidearm. Except one escaped. "Must've been a big animal to half fill the cooler."

"Mark!" Nicole snapped. "It's water, Pru. The semen, if there's any, will be in the straws."

"Really? How do—how?"

I glanced at Nicole. "All yours. Seems like something you know about."

She glared at me. "Pru, if it's all right with you, I'd like to take the cooler with me to get it forensically tested?"

"Yes, dear, of course."

She looked at me. "Come on, dad, you carry."

"Is there something wrong with you?" I asked.

"There will be with you if you keep following the path you're on."

I bent down and picked it up. Nicole slapped me on the arm. "Gloves, Jim."

"You know that joke is getting old, right?"

"It's mine and I like it," she replied, handing me a pair she had in her pocket.

I put them on and emptied the water out of the cooler, not wanting it to spill in Nicole's vehicle. It left just the bundles of straws. Nicole said, "We'll get it back to you when we're done."

Pru grimaced. "I don't think I want it back. Not after it's had that—that—bull juice in it."

"Better in the cow than a cup, Pru," I said with a grin, drawing another slap from Nicole.

"Car, now."

"Poor Pru. I should shoot you now," Nicole growled.

"Then what would you do?"

"God, I hope our child doesn't turn out like you."

"I like that," I replied.

"Like what?"

"Our child part."

She stared at my right hand. "What are you doing with that?"

I held up the straw I'd removed from the cooler. "This? I'm going to see someone about it. A vet, maybe."

She shook her head. "Try Charlie Groves. He's got a surgery on Taylor Street. I'll drop you off there if you want?"

"Sure, that would be great, thanks."

Ten minutes later, I was in the veterinary surgery

sitting waiting to see the vet. Beside me was a middle-aged woman with a Chihuahua. One of those ankle-biting little mongrels that watch you like a hawk and when you're not looking, BAM, got you. And I could tell this was such an animal because every time it looked at me, it seemed to smile, baring its fangs, a low growl deep down in its chest.

Its owner smiled at me. "He likes you."

Yeah, like a crocodile lying in wait for its next meal to come along. "I can tell. What's his name?"

"Arthur Montgomery the Third."

Shit, no wonder he was a mean little bastard. Who calls their dog something like that? The problem was he went around taking it out on someone else other than the clown who gave him the bloody name. I smiled painfully.

"You don't have a pet?" the woman inquired.

I held up the straw. "Semen."

"Oh."

"Not mine." I told her. "I can't even pee straight let alone get something like that into something like this."

She paled. "Ah...yes."

The dog leaned over and started sniffing the straw.

"No, Arthur, get away from that nasty thing."

I held it closer and let the pooch lick it.

The woman recoiled with the dog in her arms. She was about to say something when a voice said, "Mark Hayes?"

"That's me. Nice to meet you," I said standing up.

I went into the examination room where the vet awaited. He was a balding man with glasses. His head swiveled as though he was looking for something. "Where is the patient?" Groves asked me.

"I don't exactly have one," I informed him. "More like a couple of questions. Sergeant Nicole Berger said to come and see you."

He cocked an eyebrow. "She did? Who are you?"

"Mark Hayes."

Once again, my reputation had preceded me, and my name elicited the response, "*That* Mark Hayes?"

"Yes, I'm afraid so."

Groves nodded. "Nothing to be afraid of. What you did was good. Now, what can I do for you, Mr. Hayes?"

I took out the straw. "Can you tell me about these?"

"The semen straw?"

"Yes."

"What do you want to know?"

"How long do they last?" I asked.

"That depends on how they are kept. Where did you find it?"

"In a cooler of melted ice."

Groves shook his head. "There is a specific way that it should be done. Even after getting the semen into the straws. That itself is a rigorous process. If someone managed to do it and then just put it on ice in a cooler, it was doomed to fail from the start. It's meant to be kept at four degrees from the start and then lowered over a period of time to a point where it can be stored. You need a special type of freezer for that."

I nodded thoughtfully as the data processer in my head whirred and beeped. "All right. Say they were looking to sell the straw. How much would it fetch?"

"Nothing now, it's useless."

I knew that. "What if it wasn't?"

"Depending on the bull, around eight thousand a straw. How many did you find?"

I thought about the cooler. Maybe five bundles of ten. "Around fifty straws."

The vet whistled. "That's about four-hundred thousand dollars' worth of bull juice right there."

More than enough to get someone out of financial trouble.

"I'm going to become a bull and start selling my tadpoles," I said to Nicole when I got home.

"Sorry, babe, but those swimmers are all mine," she replied. "What's with that anyway?"

"Did you take the cooler to the station?"

"Not yet? Do I need to?"

"I'm not sure. Maybe."

"Do I need Rural Crimes?"

I thought for a moment. I was being paid to look into it. "No, forget it."

"What's going on, Mark? What was the quip about selling sperm?"

I grinned. "That straw, if it had viable product in it, would have been worth about eight grand. Which meant there was about four-hundred grands' worth of product in the cooler."

"Shit, Mark, I need to kick this up the chain. That's major."

"So far, it's only a stolen bull. We don't know if the semen came from said bull that's missing. Just give me time to keep looking into it. A few more days."

Nicole stared hard at me. "This could get me into trouble."

"Deny everything."

"Bloody hell."

"Have a beer—ah, maybe not."

Nicole rolled her eyes.

"Are you going to be able to work?"

"Don't, Mark," she said.

"Don't what?"

"Don't wrap me up in cotton wool already. We don't even know if I'm pregnant."

"You know," I shot back at her.

"Yeah, I do."

Later that evening I grabbed a pad and made some dot points as I tried to get things straight in my head.

- Stolen bull, fence cut, rejoined, loaded onto the back of a truck.
- Tire marks. Bridgestone M766.
- Tires: Vince Morrison, ~~Lionel White~~, Harry Poole. White lives too far away. Other two could be suspects.
- Shoe prints: Desert Tracks brand. Jim Kelly??
- Three people and a dog.
- Mason is in financial trouble. Why steal and milk your own bull?? Insurance scam??
- Stolen cooler shows up with straws of semen. From the bull?? Worth around $400,000.
- Rumors that Tom Mason isn't Jack's.

I circled back to the financial point and the straws being worth $400,000. I then scooped up my cell from beside me and apprehensively went onto the internet.

Nicole looked up from the book she was reading. Some Australian crime novel about stolen sheep or some such thing. "Do you need help with anything?"

I tucked my tongue in my cheek as I typed in a name. I was improving, but Bill Gates I wasn't. "No, I think I'm fine."

Finding what I wanted, I wrote down the phone number and then dialed.

"Hello?"

"Mister Groves, it's Mark Hayes. We met this afternoon."

"Yes, Mister Hayes. What can I do for you at this time?"

I looked at my watch. It was 9:30. "Sorry. Could you tell me if there was anyone in town who would buy semen straws?"

"Not in Friar's Lake. You might try Harry Jones at Bovine Tech in Griffith."

"OK, thanks."

I disconnected the call and made another note on my paper.

- Harry Jones, Bovine Tech, Griffith.

"I hope you don't expect to call him tonight," Nicole said.

"No."

"Good."

"Was there any word on Jim Kelly?" I asked.

"He's conscious but we haven't had a chance to talk to him yet. I'll go and see him tomorrow."

"Uh, huh."

I grabbed a new sheet of paper and made some more notes on it for the following day.

- See Vince Morrison.
- Ring Harry Jones.
- Talk to Barry Green and Jim Kelly about the cooler.
- Talk to Jack Mason.
- Talk to bank??

I stared at the notes and then up at Nicole where she sat. "You got anything you want me to do tomorrow?"

"I don't think so, why?"

"Busy day."

"That's fine, just stay out of trouble."

I wish.

CHAPTER SIX

I decided to leave talking to Vince Morrison until after I'd talked to Jack Mason again. After all, I was going to be out that way.

So, my priority was Harry Jones. I found the number and at 8:30 I made the call.

"Bovine Tech, this is Alice." Her voice was sweet, warm. I imagined her having one of those innocent faces with a broad smile coated with red lipstick.

"Hello, Alice, my name is Mark Hayes. Would Harry be in at all please?"

"I'm sorry, Mister Hayes. Mister Jones isn't in this morning. He's out of town doing a buy."

"Blast."

"Is there something I might help you with?"

I shrugged. Worth a shot. "Maybe. Has anyone from Friar's Lake approached Mister Jones about buying a batch of semen over the past week?"

"I—I can't say. Who are you again, sorry?"

"Mark Hayes. I'm a private investigator looking into what could be someone trying to sell semen straws from a stolen bull."

Alice went quiet.

"Alice?"

"We don't do anything like that." Her voice was curt.

"No, I wasn't saying that you did. I just need to see if anyone has tried to sell Mister Jones any semen straws."

"I don't know. You'll have to ask him. Is there anything else?"

I sighed. "No, I don't think so. Thank you for your time."

That went well.

Nicole surfaced from our room, ready for work. I took one look at her and winced. "You—"

"Shut up. I feel worse," she groaned. "Don't tell me I'm not pregnant."

Morning sickness. "You look lovely."

"Liar."

"Stay home."

"he criminal element in this town aren't, then neither am I."

"All right. I called Harry Jones just before and he's out of town. His receptionist was as helpful as a—"

Suddenly Nicole lurched to her feet and ran down the hallway towards the toilet. This was just the beginning of what would be a long journey.

I checked on Nicole before continuing with my day. I climbed into the Monaro and started to head out of town when I caught sight of Barry Green's van parked on the side of the street outside a house painted some out there color which reminded me of a Martian movie.

I pulled over, put the machine in park, and climbed out. As luck would have it, he was coming out to his van. "Barry Green?"

He stared at me curiously. "Who are you?"

"Mark Hayes, private investigator. Do you mind if I have a word to you?"

"I'm pretty busy. Can it wait?"

"Two minutes, no more," I assured him.

"You've got until I get an isolating switch out of the van, mate, no more."

"Thanks. You did a job at Pru Jacobs's home the other day, do you remember?"

He scratched his head through a mop of curly black hair like a dog with fleas. "Yeah, I remember."

"Do you remember seeing a cooler there?"

"Yeah, why?"

"Was it there when you left?"

"I think so."

"Jim Kelly there at the same time?"

"Jim? Yes."

"Who finished first?"

"I did. What the hell is this about?"

I smiled at him. "I'm sure it's nothing. Do you know anything about bulls?"

"Stuff all."

"Fine."

"Your time is up." He turned to leave with his switch.

"Are you and Jim Kelly friends, Barry?"

"Me and him? No, mate. Whole different circle of friends."

"OK. Thanks."

I walked back over to the Monaro and mentally crossed him off my list. That left either Jim Kelly or some random who jumped the fence and took it. My money was on Jim Kelly.

So, that's where I went next. The hospital. Jack Mason could wait.

I looked at the sign as I walked in through the sliding doors. It said something about visiting hours being after ten and some other number which I dismissed.

Innocently I started to walk past the main desk just as a stern voice said, "Where are you going, sir?"

I turned slowly and smiled at the woman who now stood with an equally stern expression on her face. But I had come prepared. Not my first rodeo. I held up the fistful of daisies, and pansies, and roses, and capeweed for all I knew. They were colorful and Mrs. Hopewell from two doors down wouldn't miss them. Not from her homegrown botanical garden.

"I have a delivery for Jim Kelly."

"Really?" She sounded skeptical.

"Yes, ma'am."

"Which florist?"

Oh, she was good. "Medallions."

She still wasn't convinced. "You've got two minutes. This could have waited until visiting hours."

"Thank you."

I started to walk off.

"Excuse me."

Shit! I turned. "Yes?"

"Would you like to know where he is?"

Double shit! "That would be great, thank you."

"Bed one, room ten. Down the end on your right."

"Thank you."

"Two minutes, Mr. Hayes."

Crap.

Jim Kelly was awake. He looked as though he'd had the shit beaten out of him, which was true, but he was still alive. I laid the flowers on the small trolley table and said, "I need to have a few words, Jim."

"Who are you?" he mumbled through swollen lips.

"Mark Hayes, private investigator."

"I don't know who it was or what they wanted." His story was succinct and rehearsed.

"I want to know about the cooler at Pru Jacobs's. The

cooler you stole and then put back with semen straws in it."

"Are you crazy?" he asked me.

I shook my head. "No. I'm just after answers. Did you milk the bull you stole?"

He reached for the call button and jammed his thumb down hard on it. "I don't know what you're talking about. Now get out."

Raw nerve. "Who helped you steal the bull?"

"Get out," he snarled, mashing the button. "You have no idea."

"No idea about what?"

"Go!"

"Ahem."

I turned and saw the director of nursing standing there. "Out."

"I'm going."

"And don't come back, Mister Hayes."

"No, ma'am."

I went outside and sat in the Monaro, going over in my head what Kelly had said to me. As luck would have it, I looked up and saw Mary from the store walking past. It looked like I wasn't the only one who'd been raiding the garden or was visiting outside of the designated hours. The flowers matched her pink dress, only if they'd been roses, the thorns would have punctured her skin the dress was that tight.

Rolling down the window I called over to her. "Mary."

Looking around, she saw me, smiled, and I waved her over. She stopped near the driver's door. "Hello, Mister Hayes."

"Nice flowers, Mary."

"Thank you. I thought they might cheer Jim up."

He'd need them. "Did Jim say what happened to him?"

"No. We haven't really talked too much though. He was still not great last night. Tired."

I nodded. "OK. Thanks."

"Welcome," she said in a chirpy voice and walked off.

I reached out and turned the key in the beast. It roared to life with a throaty gurgle. After selecting reverse, I looked in the rearview mirror before backing out of the park. Immediately I slammed it back into park, ripped the handbrake on, got rid of the seatbelt, and grabbed for the door handle. It took all a matter of seconds, and I was out of the Monaro striding purposefully towards the BMW Series 4 Coupe backed into the car park one row back.

Through the front window I could see two men. Not well, but they weren't invisible, either. I worked my way between a Holden Astra and a Mitsubishi Lancer, hooking my hip on the latter's side mirror. However, the watchers saw me coming and before I'd gone any further, the car exited the park, its wheels chirping on the asphalt. I hurriedly reached for my phone, fumbling to get the camera working.

And by the time bumble fingers had it ready to go, the two suspects were in Melbourne. "Shit. Some bloody PI you are."

I called Nicole.

"Hey, Mark. What's up?"

"I just saw the BMW you're looking for."

"Where?" Her voice was cautious, not knowing if she wanted to hear the answer or not.

"The hospital. They were in the carpark."

"What are you doing there?" she asked.

Not what happened or did they see you? What are you doing there? "I came here to talk to Jim Kelly."

"Why?" Nicole's voice became clipped.

"I needed to ask him about the cooler," I replied as a corella swooped overhead, squawking fiercely.

"You're not interfering with an ongoing investigation?"

"No, Nicole, I am not." The reply was terse. The next words were softer. "I have a theory that he was part of the group that stole the bull and milked it."

"A theory, Mark? Did he tell you anything?"

"No, but he was acting strange."

"Maybe because he just had the crap belted out of him."

"Maybe. He did say one thing though."

"What was that?" Nicole asked.

"He told me I had no idea," I replied.

"No idea about what?"

"I don't know. Matron Sloan turned up before I could get any more out of him," I told her, making reference to an old television show called *A Country Practice* which ran completely through the 80s for over 1,000 episodes.

"Matron who?"

"Never mind."

"I hope you didn't upset him."

"No," I lied.

"Did the suspects see you?" she asked.

"Maybe."

"Mark?"

"Yes."

"Shit. What happened?" Her voice was tinged with exasperation.

"They drove off."

"If you've compromised—"

"I haven't," I shot back at her through the cell, cutting her off. "These people aren't just going to go away."

"What do you mean?"

"Their type never do."

"Their type? Do we have organized crime back in Friar's Lake?"

"Maybe."

"Damn it, I have to go," she said. "And stay away from Jim Kelly. I mean it."

"Fine. I'll see you tonight."

"And, Mark, be careful."

"Always."

The Monaro chugged into the yard at Joondalup Station around eleven. I was greeted by Tom Mason who had grease up to his elbows and a black eye. "How's things?" he asked me, wiping the excess on a rag.

"I could ask you the same thing," I replied, pointing at my eye.

He nodded stoically. "One too many beers and I forgot to duck."

"Can slow your reactions down."

"Huh?"

"Beer."

"Yeah, right. You found that bull yet?"

Shaking my head, I said, "Not yet. Where's your dad?"

"In the machinery shed."

"Thanks."

I left him to his work and headed over to the large shed where I found the senior Mason working on a tractor. He looked up at me and said, "You found that bloody bull yet?"

"Not yet."

He straightened up. "Then what are you doing here?"

"Need to ask you a few more questions."

"Make it quick, I'm busy."

"All right. Are you having money problems?"

Mason stopped what he was doing and stared at me. "You don't beat around the bush, do you?"

"You told me not to. Besides, you get the best answers that way."

He nodded. "I work on the land in the middle of a drought, what the fuck do you think?"

"Was your bull insured?"

Mason smiled but the sarcasm in it was evident to see from a mile away. "You think I stole my own bull for insurance? Is that it?"

I shook my head. "I have to ask the question."

"Why?"

"Have you ever milked it for semen to sell?"

"Why would I do that?"

"Good money in it."

He stepped towards me, threatening. "There you go again, insinuating that I'm up to something."

"Just clearing away some of the loose dirt around the rabbit hole, Jack. Last time I failed to do that and dove headfirst, I had bodies piling up everywhere and people trying to kill me."

His eyes flickered. He knew exactly what I was talking about. "Why would I steal my own bull if I was going to milk it?"

"Someone had that idea."

His face changed. "What?"

"I have a cooler with semen straws in it. Looks like someone tried to milk a bull and screwed up."

"Well it wasn't bloody me," Mason growled.

"Any idea who it could have been?"

"Have you checked with Morrison yet?"

"That's where I'm going next," I replied.

"You really think it was my bull?"

I shrugged. "Maybe."

"How many straws?" Mason asked.

"About fifty."

"Do you have any idea how much money they would have fetched if done right?"

"I didn't, but I do now."

Mason nodded. "Just find the bull."

The station owner reached out to grab a spanner from the toolbox. As he did, I noticed the skin off his knuckles. "You should be more careful."

"What?"

"Your knuckles."

"Hazard of the job."

"I guess it is. I'll let you know if I find out any more."

"You do that."

Outside the shed I saw Tom talking animatedly with Betty. I couldn't hear what they were saying but she didn't look happy. Even when she saw me coming. She stormed off and went inside.

"Trouble?" I asked.

"Nothing I can't handle."

"Say, I heard you were friends with Jim Kelly. Is that right?"

Tom looked at me suspiciously. "Maybe. What if it is?"

"Any reason why someone would beat him up?"

His eyes flickered. He was about to lie to me, just like the others I'd recently talked to. "No idea."

"You seen him lately?"

"No." Another lie.

I looked down at his boots. Desert Tracks. A picture started forming in my head but quickly faded as some of the lines didn't join up with the dots. "I'll see you later, Tom."

"Yeah, sure. Where are you going, anyway?"

"To see Vince Morrison."

"What's today?"

I thought for a moment. "Wednesday."

"He won't be there. He goes to the sales on Wednesdays, takes everyone to town with him."

"I'll remember that. Thanks."

I climbed into the Monaro and left Joondalup Station. Once I reached the road, instead of turning right, I went left. If Morrison wasn't home, then it would make life easier looking around.

Next door in Outback NSW was another 5 kilometers down the rutted gravel road. The country was dry. Bone dry. Kangaroo carcasses littered the road. Most had been hit by vehicles as they came out to the roadside to find food, if there was any to be found at all.

The driveway into the Morrison place was defined by a large white rectangular arch and a line of trees on one side. I slowed the Monaro and indicated to turn left. The vehicle bottomed out in a large pothole before its nose jumped up the other side. I cursed myself for not being more careful as the car rattled across the cattle grid.

The homestead was nowhere in sight, so I assumed, like most of the houses around the place, it was perhaps another kilometer or two off the road. I still can't understand why when people put in roadways, they can't make them straight. And this one was a beauty. It swept left and right around nothing at all, and up and down through small dry washes. Ahead of me, a low ridgeline rose, covered in rocks and trees.

The Monaro gurgled as it climbed, its engine laboring. My foot went down on the pedal as I gave it more gas and it responded to the touch. As I crested the rise, my foot jammed on the brake. Ahead of me lay a large flat plain, the driveway snaking across it like a serpent gone crazy. But that wasn't what had caught my eye.

The homestead was surrounded by a carpet of green, like an island in an ocean of brown. Trees and scrub littered the plain before me, sparse but some had thicker patches. Large barns and machinery sheds were spread out around the house, and it was behind one of them that I saw the flash of blue. Someone had taken care to hide the vehicle but had not been careful enough.

I slammed the Monaro into reverse and backed hurriedly off the rise. I stomped on the brake, looked to my right, and saw a patch of brush. Putting it into drive, I turned towards it and parked the Monaro off the road.

I checked my phone and as per usual the open spaces of the outback were once again technologically free. Stuff it, I would go and look anyway. Just in case someone was in trouble.

Removing the keys, I climbed out, then went to the rear of the vehicle and opened the trunk. After my last episode, the rifle that I owned was taken away from me by the police. Now I had a Glock.

Don't worry, it was licensed. I'm not that silly. OK, matter for debate…

Using the sparse cover provided, I worked my way over the rise and closed on the homestead, using a dry creek bed to cover my approach the rest of the way. The place seemed quiet, not even a dog to be seen.

I skirted the buildings and found the blue BMW. The one which had tried to run me down. There was no one around so I tried the passenger door. It clicked and I swung it open. This was something I had done before, and in no time I'd gone through the console, the glove compartment, and looked in the back. Then I hit the trunk button.

I circled around to the rear of the vehicle and once more checked my surroundings before looking inside. My heart beat a little quicker once I realized what I was looking at. Heckler and Koch MP5s and 416s. Two of each. Whoever was with this vehicle were serious hitters. Then I realized something. These weren't anything some farmer would have which meant whoever the owners were, they were still here.

"Shit."

Now, I had friends who'd served in the armed forces and were also tactical response officers. From spending time with them, I'd come into contact with such weapons. So I unloaded the magazines from each and threw them away. I didn't say I was an expert, but that would slow them down.

You might ask why I didn't disable the car? Simple: I didn't want to trap them there with me as well. The hope was that once they were discovered they would hit the road. These were undoubtedly dangerous men.

My next move was to find out what they were up to. I walked around the rear of a corrugated iron shed escorted by a cloud of flies so thick, when you breathed in you had to clamp your teeth together to strain them out.

Suddenly my guts heaved as a small gust of thick, hot air hit me in the face carrying with it the sickly smell of rotten flesh. I looked to my right and saw the half-rotted kangaroo carcass complete with its seething mass of maggots crawling through it.

The back of my hand came to my mouth as the contents of my stomach threatened to be expelled.

Trying my best to ignore it, I moved quietly forward to the end of the shed. I paused there, listening, trying to hear anything out of the ordinary over the buzzing of the flies. At first there was nothing, then came the voices. Distant, harsh.

They were coming from a farm machinery shed further over. To get to it, I was going to have to circle the homestead and come at it from the blind side.

Running low like I was some kind of commando on a battlefield, I made my way around the building. Once I'd reached the shed, I stopped and listened to the voices inside.

"Where is the money?" one of them asked.

"I don't have it."

"Why not?" the same voice asked.

"It got stuffed up. The samples were too hot, and we couldn't sell them."

I was right about one thing.

"Not our problem. Mister Franchi wants his five-hundred grand."

Bloody hell.

"We need more time. The plan is sound."

"We need to send a message to your partner," a third gruff voice said.

"Wasn't beating Jim enough?" It had to be Jimmy Morrison.

"He was just the one who set it up. How do you think we knew where to find you?"

"But I told you what happened. We're good for the money. We just need more samples."

The whining noise of a grinder suddenly sounded from the other side of the corrugated iron wall. "Wait! Don't! I told you—"

I'd heard enough and came around the side of the shed to stand in the open where I could be seen. I saw three people. One was hooked up to the chain of a block and tackle, his arms raised in the air. His face was covered in blood from various cuts. The red fluid had run down, staining his shirt collar and front.

The other two men were big, solidly built, pug-faced mongrels who looked as though they could carry a ton of bricks on their shoulders, complete with tattoos. I brought the Glock up and said loud enough to be heard over the handheld grinder, "That's enough!"

"Who the frig are you?" the one without the grinder asked.

"I could ask you the same question."

"Fuck off, we're busy."

They seemed oblivious to the fact that I held a Glock in my hand. "I have a gun."

"So do we," said the tough with the grinder.

"Mister, you have to help me," Jimmy Morrison said urgently.

"Shut up, kid," the first man snarled before turning his gaze back to me. "I told you to leave, won't tell you again."

"You pricks already tried to run me over. How about we discuss that while we wait for the police."

The man took a step, and I fired the Glock. The bullet kicked up dirt at his feet. He stepped back, anger turning his face a deeper shade of red. "We'll remember you."

"Start walking before I shoot you in the foot this time."

The second man dropped the grinder and started to follow the other out of the shed. I should have left it at that but instead I said, "Say hi to Mister Franchi."

After they had disappeared, Morrison said, "Get me down from here."

I ignored him and followed the two toughs out of the shed and watched them walk towards their BMW. I waited until it disappeared over the rise before returning to the hanging Morrison. "You all right?"

"I am now."

Once I had him down, I helped him sit on the earthen floor of the machinery shed. "Who were they?"

"I don't know," he lied.

"What did they want?"

"I think they had me mixed up with someone else."

I stared hard at him. "I think it's time you told me what the hell is going on."

CHAPTER SEVEN

Morrison wasn't about to tell me anything, but I pushed him anyway. "Who is Mister Franchi?"

"No idea."

"He must be someone if you owe him five-hundred grand."

"Mistaken identity."

I shook my head. "Mate, I overheard you all talking. It's the reason they flogged Jim Kelly."

"I don't want to talk about it."

"What about the bull?"

"What bull?"

"The one you and Tom Mason stole from his old man," I shot back at him.

A fly landed on the rapidly drying blood on Morrison's face, and he swiped it away. "I didn't steal no bull."

I took a punt. "Sure, you did. You, Tom Mason, maybe Gerald and Bluey. Did you use your old man's truck?"

"I don't know what you're talking about."

"Yes, you do. My guess is that Tom needed the money for his old man's station. Your old man, too. But they're stubborn old bastards who look on help as a handout. So it was up to you as the next generation to get it sorted." I waved a hand. "And judging by the lack of hands around this place, I'd say your father is worse off than Joondalup Station. How am I doing?"

"Why would Tom do that? He's not even Jack's son."

Suddenly Morrison realized he'd said too much and thought about trying to cover it. But he was saved by the buzzing of my cell. I dug it out and looked at the screen, amazed I even had reception. It was Nicole. "Hey."

Her voice was unemotional. "I thought you would like to know. Jim Kelly just died."

"I'll be back as soon as I can," I replied.

"Where are you?"

"Out of town. I'll be about an hour."

"I'll see you then."

I disconnected.

"Your friend Jim Kelly just died in hospital," I said bluntly.

His expression never changed.

"That means those blokes who were here working you over, are now murderers. But I don't think that will worry them because I have a feeling they already were."

Nothing.

I nodded. "So, that's the way it's going to be?"

Again, silence.

My cell buzzed once more. I held it up. "Busy day."

Answering I said, "Yeah?"

"It's Jack Mason."

"What can I do for you?"

"I don't need your services anymore." He sounded gruff. Seemed kind of normal for him.

"Okay."

"The bull has turned up. If you come to the station whenever you're in the area, I'll pay you off."

"Fine."

"How much?"

I gave him a number.

"I'll have it ready."

"I'm not far away. I can call by."

"That will be fine."

I hung up and stared at Morrison. "I'm going. You'd better watch your back."

"Thanks for your help."

"Whatever."

"Where was it?" I asked Jack Mason.

"No idea," he grunted. "But one of the boys found him in the west hundred this morning. Only called it in a while ago."

He handed me the money he owed. "Thanks for your help."

I nodded. "Where is Tom? I'd like to see him before I go."

"Why?" Mason asked, looking up at me and placing a fist on his hip.

"No reason really."

"He was cleaning out one of the bunk rooms."

"I'll have a look."

"It's the one on the end."

"Thanks."

I walked over to the bunk house, but the door was closed. Trying the handle, it turned so I opened the door and entered the room.

Tom and Betty Mason were entwined with each other, knotted like a couple of dogs. As she flew up to get off the cot, I glimpsed her high-riding firm breasts. I turned my back to them and was about to walk out when Tom snarled, "Close the bloody door."

So, I did, but stayed facing it.

"Did you get an eyeful?" Betty asked, her voice dripping with sarcasm.

"Not what I was expecting."

"We're not related," she snapped.

"Not my place to judge."

"You can turn around now."

I about shifted my position, now facing them. Betty was stuffing a red lacy bra into her pocket while Tom was buttoning his shirt. "What do you want?"

"Just to tell you I know what happened."

"What do you mean?"

I seemed that everywhere I went people were treating me like an idiot. And I was sick of it. "You and Jimmy stole the bull to milk it, but you buggered it up. Jim Kelly was involved somehow, and maybe Betty as well. But now that the bull is back, I've been told my services are no longer required."

"That's a wild story," Betty said to me, and I could see in her eyes she'd been part of the scheme.

"I just came back from Morrison's place. Jimmy was in the process of getting beat up by the same two men who beat the shit out of Jim Kelly."

"What?" Tom asked.

That got their attention. "You heard me. They're after their boss's money."

"Shit," Tom muttered.

"Looks like this has a way to play out after all. And just so you know, Jim Kelly is dead." The way I said it was brutal, but I was beyond caring. "You'd better be prepared for more because these people won't stop until they get what they came for."

A look of horror crossed Betty's face as she glanced at Tom, but she remained silent. It was Tom who spoke. "What happened to Jim?"

"I don't know, but if I was a gambling man, I'd say it was something to do with the beating he took."

Silence.

"Are you going to tell me what happened?"

"Nothing to tell," Tom said stubbornly.

I was done. "All right, then, I'm leaving. Good luck with it."

I walked out of the bunk room and over to the Monaro. Climbing in, I turned the key, glancing at Betty Mason who now stood in the doorway staring at me. Then I put the vehicle into drive and left. For me, the job was over.

Or so I thought.

"Hi," I said to Nicole as she walked in through the kitchen doorway.

"Hi yourself," she replied and fell into my arms. "I'm tired."

"Have a seat and I'll get you a beer."

"Pregnant remember."

"Yeah."

Glancing over my shoulder, she noticed the money on the counter. "What's that for?"

"Jack Mason paid me off. His bull turned up."

Nicole raised her eyebrows, looking back at me. "Really?"

"Really."

"At least something good came from today," she said.

"What happened with Jim Kelly?" I asked.

"Blood clot went to his brain."

"From the beating?"

"The doctor thinks so, which means I've now got a murder investigation on my hands."

"Detectives from Dubbo?"

"Yes, they'll be here tomorrow."

She stepped back and kissed my lips. "I need a shower. Wash my back?"

"Sure." I gave her a grin.

Ten minutes later we were in the shower, and I was scrubbing her back with a soaped-up flannel. "That feels wonderful," she groaned.

"There's something I need to tell you."

She turned and looked at me, a water droplet on her nose. Even with her hair wet and slicked back, Nicole was beautiful. "I went out to the Morrison place today, following a hunch. When I got there, I found Jimmy being worked over by a nice couple of blokes who I presume were the same ones that beat up Jim Kelly."

"What?"

That face was no longer pretty; it was angry.

"I saw them off and they left. Then I talked to Jimmy."

"What did he say?"

"Nothing. He just clammed up."

"Shit, Mark, you should have reported this to me."

"I am now," I replied.

"You know what I mean. What else aren't you telling me?"

"Nothing," I lied. It was wrong of me, I know, but I didn't want her in the middle of this, not in her condition. Something told me that all this was about to get a whole lot worse.

"I'll go out there tomorrow and question him."

"No, Nic, leave it to the detectives."

"It's my job, Mark."

"No, it's part of a murder investigation. Leave it to the detectives."

"You know they'll want to talk to you, don't you?"

"Yeah," I groaned. "Just what I need. They still harbor

a grudge against me after what happened with the last lot of trouble we had around here."

"You'll be fine."

Later after dinner, Nicole was laying on the lounge watching some bullshit reality show, so I decided to do some more investigating to satisfy my curiosity. I sat at her computer and typed into the search engine: FRANCHI, CRIME, MOB.

Instantly I got so many hits I was feeling like a pro boxer. Salvador Franchi lived in Sydney. Supposed head of the Franchi Crime Family. "Jesus Christ."

"What was that?" Nicole asked, not looking away from the television.

"Nothing."

"Uh, huh."

I skimmed a few news articles and found out that Franchi was a person of interest in no less than five murders in Sydney. He had been tried for the import of narcotics from Mexico and Colombia and had gotten off both times. The murders were another story. Although he was suspected of being behind them, there was no concrete evidence that the police could find. Witnesses died, along with one investigating officer.

These kids were pissing in somebody's pool they had no right to be in. The Franchi family were next-level hitters.

It just confirmed what I was doing was best all around. I had to keep Nic out of it. For her safety and that of the baby.

But what I found didn't tell me how Tom Mason and the others could come into contact with Franchi. I turned to Nicole. "Do the kids around here go to high school in town or elsewhere?"

She gave me a funny look. "They can do up to ten

here in Friar's Lake, but if they want to go further, they have to go away."

"Dubbo?"

"Mostly. Some go to Sydney. Why?"

"Just curious."

She swung her legs around and placed her feet on the floor. "I know you better than that, Mark Hayes. Spill."

"Just a new case I'm working on."

"A new case?" She sounded doubtful. "Why don't I believe you?"

"My client asked to keep it on the quiet. If I start spilling everything I know to my copper girlfriend I'm going to be out of a job."

There was a knock on the door. I looked at Nicole. She gave me a 'would you get that' smile. "I'll get that, shall I?"

"You're a darling."

"And your tit is hanging out." It wasn't but it made her look.

When I opened the door, the last person I expected to be facing was Betty Mason. "I need to talk to you."

"You'd better come in."

"No, out here. I don't want your cop girlfriend to hear."

"All right." I turned my head. "It's for me. I'll just be outside."

"Okay."

I went out and closed the door. Betty looked scared. "You can't tell anyone about this."

"About what?"

"About what I'm going to tell you."

"That depends."

She took out a wad of cash and stuffed it in my hand. "That's five hundred dollars. For the next hour you work for me."

"It doesn't usually work that way."

"It does now."

I sighed. "Tell me what you want to, and I'll decide—"

My words stopped mid-sentence as my gaze fell on a dark Ford Explorer SUV parked across the street. "Bastards."

Betty turned and glanced in the same direction. "You know that vehicle?"

"Yeah."

I started walking along the path towards the front gate. Not one of my smarter moves for no sooner had my hand touched the gate, gunfire exploded from the lowered rear passenger window of the SUV.

I hit the concrete path with my shoulder as bullets cracked overhead. Then with the squeal of tires it was over, and the SUV was gone.

The sound of screaming in my ears was the last thing I expected to hear from Betty Mason, yet it was all I could hear. I ran to her side as she hunched over in a ball. "Are you okay?"

My arm went around her trembling body. "Betty, are you alright?"

"I—I don't—"

The door opened and I looked up to see Nicole emerge from the house. The expression on her face was one of shock. She lurched forward and stared at me.

"Mark?"

She was falling as I moved, barely managing to catch her, her top already turning red with her blood. "No! No! No! No! Come on, Nic, not now."

I lay her gently on the ground and she looked up into my eyes. "Mark, the—the baby."

Then her eyes closed, and she went quiet.

I was questioned by detectives for the next two days, telling them all I knew about those behind the shooting. Most of what I knew.

"How do you know it was them?"

"I know."

"Have you ever seen them before?" the big detective named Fred Waters asked me.

"Yes. The day they tried to run me over after they beat Jim Kelly."

"The young man that died?"

"That's him."

"So it's possible that they were after you and not Sergeant Berger?"

Of course they fucking were. "More than likely."

"Why would that be?"

"Possibly because I could identify them."

Waters nodded. "Considering that you gave us a good description I'd say they were right. Do you know who they might work for?"

"No."

"Why they're in town?"

"No."

He stared at me. "Mister Hayes, do you know who they are?"

"No, do you?"

"We have an idea," Waters allowed.

"Who are they?"

"Pete Ferris and Toby Knight. They're the kind of blokes you don't want to muck around with."

"At all," the second detective in the room said firmly, eyeing me sternly.

I turned my head to look at her, catching the look. Detective Sergeant Naomi Such had long dark hair in a ponytail and wore a pants suit. "They shot my pregnant partner."

"We're sorry about that, but you need to stay out of this until we work out what is going on."

"Did you talk to Betty Mason?"

"Yes, she claims to know nothing. She said she was just there visiting."

"Who do they work for?" I asked.

"Who?"

I rolled my eyes. "The fucking elves, who do you think?"

"That'll do, Hayes," Waters cautioned me. I knew who they worked for, but I wanted confirmation.

"Salvador Franchi," Such said.

"Who is he?"

"That's all you need to know."

I was about to say more when a knock on the interview room door made the detectives look up expectantly. When the door opened, the replacement sergeant who'd come with the detectives stepped into the room. Rob Haskins was a big man in his fifties. The expression on his face was serious. He looked at me then at Such. "Have you finished here?"

"Almost, why?"

"Someone just hijacked an armored truck shipment north of town."

CHAPTER EIGHT

From what I heard later, the armored truck had been hit side on by a prime mover, smashing it onto its side. The thieves then closed in on the vehicle while the occupants of the transport were still incapacitated.

After that, something happened and gunfire erupted. One of the guards was killed in the exchange of gunfire while another was wounded. The third was unharmed. The robbers got away with a little over $1,000,000, the takings of a full circuit undertaken by the armored guard company.

Then they just disappeared. Truck and all.

But that wasn't for me to worry about. I had more important things on my mind in Dubbo. As I walked into the hospital room, my emotions were set to overwhelm me when I saw Nicole.

She gave me a tired smile. "Hey."

I kissed her cheek and stepped back. "How are you feeling?"

"Not too bad. Tired."

I hesitated. "The baby?"

"It's fine. We were both lucky."

Relief. I wanted to speak but found that I couldn't so swallowed instead.

"What's wrong?" she asked.

"This is my fault, Nic. I have put your lives in danger. They were after me. I could have lost you both."

Her hand squeezed mine. "But you didn't. I don't blame you, Mark."

"You should."

She changed the subject. "How are things at home?"

"You leave and things go to crap," I told her. "Someone knocked over an armored truck north of town."

"Oh, dear."

I stared at her, knowing what she wanted to ask. "They haven't found them yet, Nic."

She nodded. "But you know who they are, don't you?"

I nodded. "Some thugs who work for a Sydney criminal called Salvador Franchi."

"Promise me you won't do anything stupid, Mark."

Silence.

"Mark?" Her tone was stern.

"I won't do anything *really* stupid," I replied, the emphasis being on really.

"Stay with me?"

I nodded and sat down.

Later that day, Nicole slipped into a coma, and I got mad.

For the next two days I sat by her side and didn't move, making sure that everything was done that could be done to ensure Nicole's recovery. But even though she was stable, she didn't wake up.

A week went by and all I got from the doctor was that the baby was fine, and Nicole would wake up when she was ready. He said that sitting by her side day after day wasn't going to make things go any faster. He said I should go back to Friar's Lake and do whatever I did for a living. Maybe come back and visit once a week.

Once a week? It sounded like they didn't expect her to wake up at all. But he was right about one thing; I couldn't do anything for her sitting there. Even though my face was the first that I wanted Nicole to see when she woke up, it could be days, weeks, or months. So I decided to do the one thing I was good at. Investigate.

I was about to leave the hospital when I heard a voice outside in the hallway. A woman's voice. "I'm here to see Nicole Berger."

I frowned and waited.

When she entered the room, I gasped. It must have been audible because she stared straight at me. It was as though Nicole had just walked into the room. "Who are you?"

My mind was still processing what was happening. "Me?"

"Yes, you."

The woman wore a pants suit and had her hair cut in a bob. She was pretty like Nicole, but her facial expressions were as though she'd been sucking lemons. "I'm Mark," I replied.

"Mark who?"

"Mark Hayes, Nicole's partner."

The woman looked down her nose at me. "She never mentioned you."

"She never mentioned she had a twin either."

"Well, she does."

"I can see that."

Her expression softened. "How is she doing?"

"No change. I'm sorry, if I'd have known I would have called you. Nicole never really mentioned any family."

The woman nodded. "I can understand that. We never really saw eye to eye on much. A conflict of interest. She puts them away and I get them out. I'm a defense lawyer. My name is Linda."

I nodded. "How did you find out?"

"The police notified me. It took me a few days to get here. I was tied up with a case in court. Now that I'm here, you can go."

I stared at her. I was leaving but she didn't know that. "What do you mean?"

"Well, as far as I'm aware, visiting is meant to be restricted to family only in cases like this. I hate to point it out, but you're not family."

Now I was starting to see why Nicole hadn't mentioned her sister. She was a bloody cow. "We live together."

"Still not family. Besides, she'll only be here another couple of days, and I'll be moving her to Sydney where she will be under the care of proper professionals. Not country quacks."

"No, she stays here."

Linda shook her head. "Being Nicole's only surviving family, I have power of attorney over whatever happens. The same as with me. You don't want to fight me on this. You will not win."

My blood pressure climbed, and memories of Tia flooded through my head, and the fights we used to have. Then came the realization that this was a fight I had no chance of winning. Maybe she was better off in Sydney. And I was better off doing what I was already going to do.

"If I give you my number, will you let me know how she and the baby are doing?"

"Baby?"

"Yes."

Her expression softened. "Of course, I will."

I wrote it on a piece of paper and handed it to her. "Please, don't forget."

"Where are you going?"

"Dark places."

I found Bomber Hansen at the pub, holding up the bar. He was on his second beer for the afternoon and when he saw me walking towards him, he stared curiously at me. "Can we have a chat?" I asked him.

"What about?"

"Business."

"Mine or yours?" he asked.

"Mine."

"How much?"

"Five grand."

"I'm in."

"You don't know what I want you to do?" I pointed out.

"Don't give a shit. If the job pays five grand, I'm in."

I stared at him, his tattoos, wondering if I'd made the right choice. "Do you know your way around Sydney?"

"Some. I haven't lived here all my life."

"Apart from Dubbo Jail," I reminded him.

"Screw you. You want my help or not?"

"Yes. Be outside here at six in the morning."

Bomber nodded. "I'll be waiting."

My next port of call was Jace to find out how the

investigation was proceeding. "How's the boss?" he asked me.

"No change."

"Shit. Hang in there, man."

"Yeah. Any news?"

"The prime mover was found burned out on Hunter Road, north of town. A farmer called it in."

"When was that?"

"Two days ago. Crime scene people found nothing. It was stolen, of course. The owner left the keys in it, and it was taken."

"Who was the owner?"

"Leave it, Mark."

"Just curious. No sign of the thugs from Franchi?" I asked.

"Nothing."

I nodded. "Thanks."

The whole experience was helpful. Not.

Suddenly Jace's radio came to life.

"You there, Jace?" Constable Jessie Murphy asked, her voice crackling.

"I'm here."

"The sergeant wants you back at the station. It looks like the SUV we were looking for has been found."

"On my way."

I started following him. He stopped. "No, Mark."

"I want to see, Jace."

"Look, you can't come with me, but I can't stop you following me out to the crime scene."

I nodded, understanding what he was saying. "See you around, Jace."

———

The SUV was nothing but a burned-out shell with a large patch of blackened grass surrounding it. It had been parked off the side of the gravel road before being torched, a long way from anywhere, which was why it had taken so long to be found.

I pulled the rumbling Monaro off the road and turned the motor off. I looked at my watch. It was around four in the afternoon.

The police were already starting to tape the scene off as I climbed out. The only ones there were Jace and Murphy. So, I slipped under and walked towards the SUV.

Jace saw me coming. "You shouldn't be inside the perimeter, Mark. The sergeant and the detectives will be here soon. If they find you here, they'll not be happy."

"I won't be long," I said to him, taking out my cell.

"Damn it, Mark," he growled at me when I started taking pictures.

Ignoring him, I kept going. "I'm going away for a few days tomorrow," I told him.

"Where?"

"Sydney."

"Anything special?"

I took another photo. "Not sure."

The car had obviously been lit using accelerant. I looked for any other clues. Murphy was already putting out her little yellow markers, so I got pictures of them as well.

In the distance I could see the rising dust cloud.

Jace said, "You need to get out, now, Mark."

I nodded and walked towards the tape. Once under I rested against my car while the new arrivals eased to a stop. Haskins climbed out of his 4X4 and stared at me. "What are you doing here?"

"Out for a drive."

"Bullshit. This investigation is off limits to you."

"If you say so."

Waters and Such climbed from their vehicle and asked me the same question.

"I was at a party up the road when I came across this here. Thought I'd hang around."

"No one likes a smartass," Such pointed out.

I nodded. "Just like they don't like stupid questions."

The pair walked past me and slipped under the tape. This left me there alone, which I wouldn't be for long. George Timmins, the local news reporter, would arrive, just as sure as the sun came up, in his early model Mercedes. But until then, I did the only thing I could do. I looked around outside the perimeter.

At first, I found nothing but dry grass, kangaroo shit, and dirt. But dirt has a way of preserving things if you can get to it before the wind springs up and blows it all away. Out here that could be hours or days.

In this instance the wind had been good to me, and I found myself standing over a clear boot print made by Desert Tracks boots. My hand dipped into my pocket and came out with my cell. I took a picture and put it back.

"Hey!"

I looked up and saw Such staring at me. I said nothing and she started walking in my direction.

"What are you doing?" she asked me as she slipped under the tape.

"Not much."

"What did you take a picture of?"

I pointed at the ground. "Boot print."

Such looked down at it. She frowned. "All right, I'll bite. What's so special about it?"

I gave her a quizzical look. She sighed. "Indulge me."

"Boot print was made over the past few days. Any longer than that and it would have blown away."

"You think it was made by whoever dumped the SUV?"

"Might be."

"But what happened to Sergeant—"

"It doesn't mean they couldn't have hung onto it and then dumped it," I said, cutting her off.

"Granted."

"Trust me, this vehicle hasn't been here that long."

She looked thoughtfully at me and nodded. "All right."

Such then turned and ordered Murphy to move the tape. With that done she turned back to me and held out her hand. "What?" I asked.

"Phone."

"No."

"Give me your phone or I'll lock you up for obstructing a police investigation."

Muttering under my breath I handed it over. She flicked through my photos and deleted them as she went. She returned it to me and said, "It might help if you had a PIN number to lock it."

I looked at the empty folder. "No point now is there?"

She shrugged. "I guess not."

I turned away and as I did so I heard her say, "Stay away from the investigation."

Without turning I extended my arm and lifted my middle finger.

I was about to climb into the Monaro when Timmins arrived. He climbed out of his Mercedes and hurried across to me. "What's news, Mark? Is there anyone in it? Do they know who stole it?"

"No."

"Blast, I was hoping you might know something. How is Sergeant Berger?"

"Still the same."

"I'm sorry to hear that." The reply was genuine even though he and Nic had a combative relationship.

"Hey, Tim, do you know who owns the SUV?"

His eyes came alive with excitement as he said, "Not for sure but word is that the owner is Stan Collier."

"Where's he from?"

"Hampton."

"Thanks."

The Monaro slowed to a stop outside the pub early the following morning. True to his word, Bomber Hansen was waiting for me. He climbed in. "What, no bag?" I asked.

"Don't need one," he grunted. "If I need clothes, I'll get them there."

"Fine."

I pulled away and pointed the nose of the vehicle towards the edge of town. We'd drive the some three-hundred kilometers to Dubbo and get a plane from there to Sydney.

"You never told me what you want me to do, exactly," Bomber said after we passed the welcome sign.

"I need you to watch my back."

"From who?"

"Bad people."

"You're going to have to give me more than that," Bomber said.

"Salvador Franchi."

"Pissing in a big-fish pond. Not a smart move."

"That's why I'm bringing you along."

"Do you have a gun?"

"No." It wasn't exactly a lie. I wasn't taking the Glock with me.

"That's fine, I'll get us a couple when we get there," Bomber replied.

"No, no guns."

"My friends can get them."

"What friends?"

"Bikers I know."

"What bikers?"

"Taipans."

Taipans. One of the fastest growing Motorcycle Clubs on the east coast. Known for bringing drugs into the country from Mexico and Colombia. Selling illegal firearms and stand over tactics.

"No guns," I said again.

"All right," Bomber said with a nod. "But I want to know what it is I'm getting myself into."

I swerved the Monaro around a kangaroo carcass on the road. "Fine. I'm looking for two men. Two of Franchi's men. I believe they are responsible for shooting Nicole."

"Why would they do that?"

"Because the bullets were meant for me." I went on to tell him the backstory.

"And you think that it was because you trod on their toes?" Bomber asked.

"Yes."

"What are you going to do if and when you find them?"

"I don't know."

"I'm not killing anyone for you," he said. "I draw the line at killing. Beat the shit out of someone, sure, but not murder. I've just got out of prison."

I slammed the brakes on, and the Monaro skidded to a halt. "What? No! No, no killing. I just want you to make sure no one tries to kill me."

"Just so we understand."

"Yes."

We reached Dubbo and waited an hour to catch QANTAS flight 436 to Sydney. Bomber got himself a pie and Coke, man after my own heart, and sat eating it. Once he was done, he let out a loud burp and said, "Fuck, that was good."

A middle-aged woman sitting not far from him glared over her glasses at him. He shrugged broad shoulders. "What are you looking at?"

She shook her head and went back to the magazine she was reading. I said to him, "Take it easy."

"Whatever."

For some reason I couldn't explain, Bomber had me on edge. Sure, he'd agreed to help me, but I was still uneasy. And it didn't improve when twenty minutes before we were due to depart, two detectives appeared.

"Hey, Bomber, long time no see," the first detective said.

"Been in jail?" the second asked.

"Very funny," Bomber growled. He looked at me. "Mark, meet C and C. If you're wondering what their names are, it's Cocks and C—"

"That's enough," the first detective said.

"—unts."

"Do you gentlemen have a problem?" I asked.

"When we heard Bomber here was flying out of Dubbo, we thought we'd come and wave him off," the second detective said.

"Who are you?" the first asked me.

"Hayes. You blokes got some ID?"

"What for?"

"Because I don't know you from Adam. You might

say you're detectives, but you might just be a couple of male strippers looking for a place to blow each other."

Bomber burst out laughing. The only one as it turned out. Both detectives reached for ID.

"Cox and Curtis," I read out loud. "You obviously have history with Bomber."

"Pricks arrested me the last time I went to jail."

"Don't tell me, they set you up?"

Bomber snorted. "Fuck no. I was done fair and square trafficking a shit ton of drugs. Did three years for it. Got five but I was a good boy."

"Rooting the warden would be my guess," Cox said.

"Your missus before I went in," Bomber shot back at him.

It was like dealing with children.

"Is there something else you want?" I asked them.

"Take some advice," Curtis said to me. "Watch your back. He may act all good and friendly, but he still has ties to the old crew and that will get you killed."

"I'll take it under advisement."

"You do that."

They walked away, and beside me I heard Bomber say, "Assholes."

I turned to him. "You want to tone it down a bit?"

"What?"

"Just take it easy."

He grumbled and was about to say something when I guess he thought of the five grand I was going to pay him, so he changed his mind.

We boarded the plane and the flight to Sydney was uneventful. From the airport we took a cab to a hotel in town called the Oberon. It wasn't a flash five-star job, but it was comfortable enough for our purposes. We had separate, side by side rooms which I paid for. Then an hour after we arrived, Bomber came to me and said, "The mini bar is empty."

"Maybe they forgot to fill it."

"No, it was full, just not anymore."

"Shit, Bomber, what the hell?"

"I was thirsty," he said with a shrug.

"Yeah, well don't have any more. I need to find Franchi."

"I might be able to help out with that," he told me. "Let me make a few calls."

So, while he went to work making calls, I went outside onto the balcony which was nestled twenty floors above the pavement.

I guess I'd been in the country too long for all of a sudden, the sights and smells I'd once been used to in the city were foreign to me. Exhaust fumes, car horns, city lights, and a thousand other sounds and smells. Nothing like the fresh country air, flies, and dust storms.

My cell buzzed. I answered. "Hello?"

"It's me, Linda."

"How is Nicole?" I asked immediately.

"She's still the same," she replied. "We're in Sydney. She's under the care of a good specialist."

"The baby?"

"Still fighting like its mother."

I let out a sigh of relief.

"Listen," she continued. "The reason I called is that they did some scans this afternoon and they found a bleed on her brain. They had to open her skull to relieve the pressure."

I started to panic. "Is she going to be all right?"

"The doctor said it looks positive, but we won't know for sure until tomorrow."

I remained silent.

"Mark, are you there?"

"Yes."

"Did you hear me?"

"Yes."

"Is there anything you want to know?" Linda asked.

"Just that she'll be all right."

"I'll call you tomorrow when I know more."

"Thank you."

The sliding door behind me opened. I turned and Bomber came out. "Franchi spends his evenings at a restaurant, about five blocks from here. He should be there now."

I nodded. "Then we'd better get ready for dinner and go see him."

CHAPTER NINE

The restaurant fronted a busy four lane road with shops and metered parking on each side. Neon signs flashed incessantly advertising whatever was within the store they hung above. Even the prostitutes were out on the corners trying to accost us as we walked to our destination.

It was something I'd become used to in Melbourne, so it wasn't much of an eye-opening experience. On one corner I saw the sleight of hand used with a drug deal going down. I looked at Bomber and he shook his head. "Sloppy pricks."

As we crossed an intersection where a narrow foot alley emerged onto the main thoroughfare, I happened to glance in as we went by. I saw a man in a suit standing, his pants open. Before him knelt a prostitute, her head moving rhythmically back and forth as she worked his shaft with her mouth.

Again, something I was already used to.

By the time we reached the restaurant I was starting to feel at home.

The flashing sign above the door gave it the name,

Reggie's. We walked inside and were greeted by the maître d'. "Can I help you, gentlemen?"

"We'd like a table for two?"

The man's eyes went straight to Bomber. "Do you have a reservation, sir?"

"No."

"Then I'm afraid I have no tables available."

A man in a suit escorting a thin brunette with a low-cut gown walked past us. Bomber asked, "What about them?"

"They are regulars, sir."

"So they just get to walk straight in?"

The man made no reply.

I stared at him before saying, "Tell Mister Franchi that Mark Hayes is here to see him."

That got his attention. He disappeared and came back a few minutes later. He said, "Mister Franchi says he doesn't know you. Good evening."

We left. There was nothing else to do. We began retracing our footsteps and hadn't gone far when a black SUV pulled up beside us and the front passenger window went down.

"Hey."

We both stopped and looked at the face filling the opening. "What?"

"Mister Franchi wants to speak to you."

Bomber and I started towards the vehicle. The man said, "Just you. Not him."

I glanced at the big man beside me. He shrugged. "All right. Bomber, I'll meet you back at the hotel."

"You got it."

I climbed into the back and found a gray-haired man wearing a dinner suit sitting opposite me. He stared at me for a long moment before speaking. In that time, I'd contemplated killing him, but I needed answers. He said, "You are Mark Hayes?"

"And you are Salvador Franchi."

"What can I do for you, Mister Hayes?"

The SUV pulled out into the traffic. "Where are we going?"

"Not far. Now, back to the question."

"Tell me about loaning money to a man called Tom Mason."

He frowned. "Are you a policeman, Mister Hayes?"

"No, I'm a private investigator."

Franchi hesitated as he thought about answering. "I've heard the name but never had dealings with him."

"Are you sure?"

"I think I would know."

"What about Jim Kelly and Jimmy Morrison?" I asked.

"Jim Kelly, I know. Morrison I've never met, like Tom Mason."

"How do you know Jim Kelly?"

"He went to school with my son," Franchi explained.

"Did you know he was dead?"

He stared at me. "No."

"He died from injuries received from a beating handed out by two of your men. Ferris and Knight."

"Who told you this?" he asked.

"I saw them."

"Marlon, stop the car."

The SUV pulled over and stopped. "Get out, Mister Hayes."

"I'm not done, yet."

"Yes, you are."

The door opened and a large man stood there holding it. "I still have questions."

"I will talk to you again tomorrow, Mister Hayes. Good night."

I stood on the sidewalk and watched the vehicle pull away into the traffic.

I found Bomber Hansen sitting in the hallway waiting for me, ass on the floor, back to the wall. His coat was off, and his tattoos exposed. I saw the snake twisting around his forearm. It was the first time I'd ever taken a lot of notice of them. He looked up at me. "You all good?"

I nodded. "Yeah, still in one piece."

He got up off the floor and his shirt opened a touch, and I noticed the handgun tucked into his waistband. I pointed at it. "What's that?"

"Insurance," he grunted. "Lot of pricks in Sydney still don't like me."

"Is that why you're out at Friar's Lake?"

"Partly."

I opened my door, and we went inside. I grabbed a beer from the mini bar and one for Bomber. Twenty bucks gone just like that. He took a sip and said, "What did he want?"

"He asked questions, and I asked questions, and he told me nothing."

"Nothing unusual there."

Shaking my head, I said, "No, it was as though he knew nothing about it."

Bomber drank some more and swallowed. "Someone stuffed up."

I nodded. "Could be. Either that or he doesn't want to talk. I'll find out tomorrow."

"How's that?"

"He said he would see me again."

"Does he know where we are staying?" Bomber asked, a flicker of concern coming to his face.

"I guess we'll find out." I paused. "How did you get the gun?"

Bomber glared at me. "My business."

"All right."

He grunted again and said, "I'm going to bed. See you in the morning."

I watched him close the door and eyed the light and shadows in the gap. He turned left. His room was to the right.

"Shit."

I followed him out onto the street and for a further five blocks before we hit Hawkins Street. There was a time once when Kings Cross had been the hub of crime and all things sinful. Now it was Hawkins Street, the new hub.

One could walk fifty meters and purchase any quantity of a variety of drugs from various dealers. Instead of one dealer, one patch, it was now one dealer, one specialty. Ecstasy, the bad stuff, not like the way it was back in the nineties. Coke, heroin, uppers, downers, green pills, blue pills, meth, and anything else you could think of. The dealers had an understanding. There was more than enough to go around. Young people, and old, were hooked up even more than what they used to be.

Behind the supply were three factions: Taipans Motorcycle Club, the Asian Crime Syndicate, and Salvador Franchi. Only the Taipans had a base on site. They were the only ones who didn't give two shits about the law peering in on them despite the no fraternization laws.

They operated out of a nightclub. The Pink Palace, however, was a little more than that. Downstairs, booze and drugs were sold, upstairs was the brothel. Illegal? Yes. Shutdown? No. At this time, the Drug and Firearms Squad and Organized Crime Squad were working under the one umbrella. One allowing corruption to run rife within. There was too much money to be made looking the other way. While things were peaceful, anyway. But as with fine lines, all it took was for one to be crossed and everything went to shit.

A line crossed in Melbourne some ten years previously when a bloody shootout had occurred on a strip controlled by two rival drug gangs. Five men had died that night along with three innocent bystanders.

The aftermath, however, rocked the whole of Victoria Police. One man spilled a name, and the dominoes began to fall. It was only a matter of time before it happened here. After all, the criminal enterprises holding a little slice of the pie inevitably wanted more.

Bomber stopped outside the Pink Palace, greeted by two men just as big and heavily tattooed as he was. As they talked, I brought up my cell and took pictures of them. Then they disappeared inside.

I stood across the street, deciding whether to follow him inside. The sensible side argued no, but the PI side always won out in the end, and I stepped out onto the street and started across.

"You got a ticket?" the security guy on the door asked me grudgingly.

"Bomber said I didn't need one."

"Who the fuck is Bomber?" he growled.

"Are you going to give me that bullshit?" I asked. I was playing a dangerous game.

He just stared at me.

I decided to push it a little harder. "Bomber Hansen. You know who I mean, now?"

"Nope."

"Let him pass, Frog."

I stared at the figure in the doorway. Bomber stood staring at me. The man called Frog stepped aside and I followed Bomber inside.

The music within was loud but not "doof-doof" loud. We stopped at the bar and were served by a young lady wearing a bikini top and cut-off jeans revealing her ass cheeks. Every scrap of exposed flesh was covered by multiple tattoos. Through the tight bikini top, I could make out the piercings through each of her nipples. Black eyeshadow was painted heavily around blue eyes.

"What'll it be, Bomber?" she asked.

"Two beers, Shandy," he replied. "Draught."

"You got it."

While we waited, I looked around the club from where I stood. At the center was a vertical stainless-steel pole affixed to the ceiling. Giving it a solid workout was a slender blonde with large breasts and wearing a skimpy thong.

Circled around it were rows of seats, most occupied, some vacant. Then there were the tables and booths. Again, some vacant. Those occupied were by girls giving patrons lap dances or blowjobs under the table.

Shandy brought the beers and Bomber passed one over to me. I took a pull and he said, "You following me, Hayes?"

I stared at him. "When a bloke is working for me, tells me one thing, and does exactly the opposite, it tends to make me curious."

He nodded. "Fair enough. I can see that."

"So, what are you doing here?"

He glared at me, fire in his eyes. "That has nothing to do with you."

"You forget you're working for me, Bomber?" I asked him. "Yet here you are back with the old crew."

"I'm not with the old crew anymore," he replied. "Not since prison."

"So why here?"

"Catching up with old friends," he replied.

"Same old friends who gave you the gun?"

He stared at me and took another drink.

One of the waitresses came up to him and ran a hand across his shoulders. She leaned in without a word and kissed him on the lips. It reminded me of an anaconda trying to devour its prey, except this one was trying to reach the big man's tonsils with her tongue.

When they parted, she looked at him misty-eyed and said, "Hey, Bomber."

"Hey, Candy."

She turned and looked at me. "Who's your friend?"

"His name is Mark."

"What does Mark do?"

"He's a PI."

She stared at me and then said, "Uh, huh."

"No, you can't have him."

Candy pouted. "Pity, I have a feeling he could make a girl like me scream."

"How about I make you scream later?" Bomber asked her.

"Hell, yes," she said excitedly. "I'll make your eyes pop, baby."

Frigging hell, what was this shit?

Another kiss and she was gone.

"Old friend, huh?"

A grin split his whiskery face. "Old screw. Goes off like a stick of dynamite."

"She seems kind of, ah, eager."

"Mate, she'd root anything that moved, and if it didn't, she'd give it a shove." He laughed out loud but there was no humor in his eyes.

I drank some more before Bomber said, "I have to go see a friend. Stay out of trouble."

Bomber weaved a path through the tables towards one at the rear where three men sat. They all shook hands, and he took his seat.

"You want another beer, Champ?"

Turning, I saw Shandy staring at me impatiently. "Maybe?"

"Not a hard question to answer, yes, or no?"

"Why not?"

I watched her walk away, my eyes drawn to her tight butt cheeks. I smiled wryly and shook my head. When she returned with the beer, she placed it on the drip mat and said, "Ten bucks."

My eyebrows shot up. "Are you for real?"

"Do I look like I'm laughing?"

"No, I guess you're not."

She went to walk away but before she could I asked her, "Who is that over there that Bomber is talking to?"

"Screw you," she said and walked off.

"Nice talking to you."

I still had one way of finding out. Worked my way towards them and sat in a seat near the pole dancing stage. I managed to get a couple of pictures, but I'd check them out later. In the meantime, I tried to blend in by drinking my beer and watching the dancers.

"You want a lap dance, honey?"

I looked up to see a thin, athletic looking girl smiling encouragingly at me. Shaking my head, I said, "No, thanks."

"If you're worried about an audience, I can take you somewhere more private."

"I'm fine."

She leaned in close and said, "Mister, if you want to see this night out, you'd better get up and follow me."

I stared at her and there was an urgency in her eyes. "All right."

She took my hand and led me across the room to a double door then out through it. We traversed a carpeted hallway and to a private lounge out the back. "What is this all about?"

She turned to face me. Through the heavy makeup I could make out the freckles on her face. "You need to get out of here."

"Why?"

"Because there are some bikers who are talking about kicking the shit out of you."

This came as a surprise. "Me? Why?"

"Because they can. Shit, I don't know why. Do they need a reason?"

"Why are you telling me this?"

"Because I don't want to see you killed which is exactly what will happen if Meat and Donger get hold of you."

"Don't they know I'm here with Bomber Hansen?"

"That doesn't matter. Bomber isn't part of the Taipans at the moment. He used to be their sergeant-at-arms."

"What do you mean at the moment?" I asked.

"He's—"

The door opened and interrupted her words. I stared at the opening and watched two burly men enter the room. No doubt they were Meat and Donger. One had a goatee and the other a shaved head. Both wore sleeve tattoos and looked mean.

"You blokes are making a mistake," I told them.

"The only mistake has been made by you, cunt," the bigger of the pair said. "You don't fucking belong here."

"Is that really a nice way to talk to someone you've just met?" I asked as I edged towards a table with a lamp sitting on top of the polished wood.

"Shut the hell up."

This was going to go one of two ways. They would beat the shit out of me, or I would give them a few lumps and then they would still beat the shit out of me. I glanced at the girl who had tried to save me from the fate I was about to endure. "You'd best leave."

She hurried out of the room, giving the two hairy-assed bikers a wide berth. Once more I tried to reason with them. "Can we do this one at a time? If I'm going to push you around with my face I would rather do it that way."

They grinned and one of them stepped forward. I think it was Meat. He was the bigger of the two. When he was close enough, I moved with all the speed I could muster. I scooped up the solid lamp and smashed it against his head.

The biker went down in a heap on the floor, blood soaking into the carpet from the gash in his head. I dropped what remained and stared at the other biker.

"You rotten bastard," he snarled at me and stepped forward.

In a fight for survival, one does what one can to try to secure the outcome in their favor. I did what he least expected. I went at him, hard.

I had already landed two blows before the big man realized what was happening. He jerked, taken aback by the ferocity of my blows. It gave him pause and it also gave me an opening to press home my attack.

My right foot lashed out impacting alongside the knee. The big man's leg buckled, and I heard a sickening pop as the ligaments went.

He cried out in pain as he crashed to the floor, a giant tree in an old growth forest. But I wasn't done. I was mad now and blinding rage started to cloud my judgement. I stepped in and kicked him in the head. Three times.

I was lining up for the fourth when I felt rough hands grab me and drag me away from the now bleeding man who lay still. "Easy, tiger, I think he's had enough."

Bomber Hansen released me, and I whirled to face him. He held up both hands and said, "Calm down, you've done for them."

"What was this bullshit?" I snarled at him.

"It had nothing to do with Bomber," a different man said, stepping past my supposed friend.

"Who are you?" I asked curtly, still pissed at what had happened.

"I'm Jim. The boys call me Mongrel."

He said it like it was meant to mean something to me. I just stared at him and waited for him to expound on the statement. He looked mean and important at the same time.

He said, "Taipan's club president."

I indicated to the two fallen men. "So this is your doing?"

He shook his head. "If it was, the job would have been done proper."

"Yeah, right."

He sighed impatiently. "Time for you to go."

"My thoughts exactly."

"I'll have a ride for you outside."

"I don't ride," I replied.

He smiled. "Not all bikers ride bikes all the time."

He disappeared and I looked at Bomber. "What the bloody hell was this?"

He shrugged. "Looks like you handled the situation."

"Why are you here, Bomber?"

"Just saying hello."

I shook my head as I walked off. "Whatever."

CHAPTER TEN

I spent most of the next day sitting around the hotel room, watching old movies on the TV. That was until a knock on the door about three revealed two men in suits standing there. Cops. Detectives.

"Are you Mark Hayes?"

"Who wants to know?"

"Can we come in?"

"Who are you?"

They flashed their badges. "How about now?"

I stepped aside and they entered.

Closing the door behind them I asked, "What is this all about?"

They were both slim men, one a little taller than the other. He was the one who spoke. "I'm Detective Inspector Walsh. This is Detective Sergeant Jackson. We're from New South Wales Police. I believe you know Stewart Higgins."

"We've met." Higgins was the copper who'd interrogated me after the ruckus I got mixed up in at Friar's Lake when I was looking for Trent Jacobs.

"Would you mind telling us what you were doing with Salvador Franchi last night?"

"Working a case," I replied, not lying.

"That's right," Jackson said. "You're a PI."

I nodded. "Being a cop didn't work out for me."

"Too much authority."

"Too many wankers," I fired back at him.

"What is the case?" Walsh asked me.

"If I told you that I would be breaking client privilege."

"Piss off," Jackson said.

"I'm trying to find out who shot my partner," I snapped. "Is that what you wanted to hear?"

"Stay away from Franchi unless you want to be charged for interfering with an ongoing investigation."

I just nodded. No point in telling them I was expecting to see him later that afternoon. "Why is Professional Standards knocking on my door and not Organized Crime?"

"You don't have to worry about that," Walsh said.

"Still got crooks in the ranks, huh?"

"What makes you think that Franchi is involved?"

"His muscle was getting around Friar's Lake at the time. I had a difference of opinion with them. Next you know the place is getting shot up and Nicole is in hospital with a bullet wound. Put two and two together and you get four."

"The toughs you're talking about, were they Toby Knight and Keg Ferris?"

"That's them," I replied.

"You won't find them in Sydney," Jackson said. "They disappeared a while back and haven't been seen since."

"Really?"

"Really."

"Now, let's get to the next item we need to discuss," Walsh said to me. "Bomber Hansen."

"What about him?"

"What's he doing with you?"

"Watching my back."

Jackson grunted. "Waiting to put a knife in it more likely."

"What is it with you pricks?" I snapped at the detective sergeant. "Watch too many hard-boiled crime movies? Good cop, bad cop."

Walsh started to speak when my cell rang. "Don't answer it, we haven't finished."

"Yes, we have," I shot back at him and answered the call. "Hayes."

"Corner of Mullet and Fisher in an hour. Be there."

The call disconnected and I pocketed the cell. "I have to go out. Have a nice day."

They weren't happy, but they left anyway.

A few moments later, Bomber knocked on my door. "What did the pigs want?"

"To ask me what I was doing with Salvador Franchi."

"That would be right, eyes everywhere, the bastards."

"I have to go out to meet with Franchi," I told Bomber.

"Give me a minute and I'll get ready."

"No, he won't let you ride with us anyway. If I'm not back by tomorrow, then head back to Friar's Lake."

"What about my money?"

"Nicole will pay you if something happens to me."

"She better. I'm not—shit, if she ever wakes up."

"She will. Now, are you going to be here when I get back?" I asked.

"We'll see."

The same SUV as the previous night picked me up on time. I climbed in and found Franchi waiting for me. "You are punctual. I like that."

"Habit, I guess."

"I have some answers to your questions. Some of those might lead to more questions. We'll start with the money. My son loaned his friend four-hundred thousand dollars. With the interest that I charge it came to an even five hundred. The loan has been paid."

"When?"

"Two days ago." He picked at a speck of lint on his suit.

"What about your men? Did your son tell them to take me out?"

"No."

"Can you be sure of that?" I asked him.

Franchi glared at me. "One thing my son will not do, Mister Hayes, is lie to me. He would not dare."

I studied him for a moment. "There's something you're not telling me."

"My son sent those men out to Friar's Lake to collect a debt that was owed when the deadline came and went. They—"

"They beat up a bloke and he died."

"Unfortunately. But I only have your word for that."

"It's true."

Franchi shrugged. "It does not matter anyway. It would seem that the two men that my son sent have disappeared."

"As they would with the police chasing them," I pointed out.

"You don't understand, Mister Hayes. Nobody knows where they are. They vanished before the shooting."

"That's almost two weeks ago. Why are you telling me this?"

"Because I want you to find them for me. I'll pay you twenty thousand dollars."

I chuckled. "You're crazy."

He reached inside his coat for an envelope. "I will pay you half up front."

"What is the alternative?"

"The alternative is that I send my own people to look, and they won't be as discreet about it as you will be."

"What if I don't find them?" I asked.

"I've heard of your exploits, Mister Hayes. I'm certain you will."

I hesitated before taking the money. I stuffed the envelope inside my shirt and tried to figure out the one question which still hadn't been answered. Who was it that tried to kill me?

When I returned to the hotel, I found Bomber waiting for me. "How did it go?"

"I'm not sure."

"What do you mean?"

I dug out the envelope full of cash and opened it. I took out five grand and passed it over.

"What's this?" Bomber asked incredulously.

"That's your five grand."

"Where did you get that from?"

"Franchi."

"Why would he give you that much cash?"

"To find two missing men," I replied. "The same ones who were responsible for the death of Jim Kelly."

"They've gone to ground, for sure."

"I guess I'll find out."

"You're taking the job?" Bomber asked me.

"Don't have much choice, do I?"

"Tread carefully, my friend."

"I intend to," I allowed. Then I said, "I'm going out again."

"You want me along?" Bomber asked.

"No, I'm just going to see Nicole."

"We leaving tomorrow?"

"If we can get a flight."

"Good, I'm wanting to get back anyway."

"Yeah, me, too."

"I see you found it all right," Linda said to me from the other side of Nicole's hospital bed.

"Yeah." I ran my gaze over Nicole. She looked so peaceful. "How is the baby?"

"Still fine."

"Thanks for letting me come," I said.

Linda smiled at me. "I'm not a complete monster."

"Just a little scary one," I said back.

"Something like that. Did you have any luck?"

"Some, not a lot. Let's say it has been interesting."

She raised her eyebrows. "Really?"

"Yes. Say, in your travels as a defense lawyer, have you come across any of the Taipans?"

"The bikers?"

"Yes."

"No," she replied with a shake of her head. "Even if I did, I wouldn't touch them. Once you're in, there's no out."

"What can you tell me about them?"

"Why? You're not involved with them, are you?"

"Not exactly."

Linda frowned at me. "Mark?"

"I have a bloke with me who used to be one. I

followed him to the Pink Palace last night and had some troubles."

"What is his name?"

"Bomber Hansen."

"I've heard of him. Used to be the sergeant–at-arms before he went to jail in Dubbo."

"What was that for?"

"Trafficking drugs, I think. You'd do best to stay away from him."

"I'm thinking that myself," I replied. "At least he's out."

"You're never out," Linda sneered. "Did you say he was out at Friar's Lake?"

"That's right."

"Ask yourself why," she said.

I must have looked puzzled because she continued, "Like I said, you're never out of the Taipans. So for him to be out at Friars Lake there must be a reason."

What she said made sense. I don't know why I didn't pick it up earlier. Maybe it's what the detectives at Dubbo were trying to tell me. I sighed.

"What are you going to do?"

"Go back to Friar's Lake and do what needs to be done." She didn't need to know the details.

"By that you mean, find out who is responsible for this?" she asked, pointing at Nicole.

"Yes."

"Do you think you will?"

"I hope so."

"What do you have?" Linda asked.

"Do you really want to know?" I asked her.

"A second perspective couldn't hurt. I bet you bounce things off Nic at home."

I nodded. "All right. It started with a missing bull and

a cooler. It wasn't long before the cooler returned with semen straws in it."

Linda pulled a face. "Gross."

"In the meantime, two thugs were getting around town looking for some people who'd borrowed money from Salvador Franchi. Only I've since found out that it was his son who loaned them the money."

"Not the type of circle you want to get mixed up in."

"It gets worse. I had a run-in with them and the next thing you know the house where Nic lives was getting shot up by men trying to take me out."

"Are you sure you were the target?"

"Almost certain."

"And the police have no idea who it was?"

"They—and I—were of the opinion that it was Franchi's thugs. But they've disappeared, according to Franchi."

"Just a story?"

"He's paid me ten grand up front to find them or their bodies."

Her eyes widened. "Shit, Mark, you're way into this now."

"Don't I know it. The original reason I came to Sydney was to find the two men responsible. But now I find out the original debt has been paid."

"What debt?"

"The one that the bull was stolen for to pay back. It was five-hundred grand all up with interest. Which brings me to another issue. Just before this money got paid, an armored truck was hit in the district and around a million was stolen from it."

"Coincidence?"

"No such thing as coincidence."

"So what you're saying is that the truck was hit to get the money to pay back the debt?"

"I think so."

Linda nodded abruptly. "Right, case solved."

"I wish it was that easy."

"Why do I sense you're not convinced?"

"Because, yes, the people I'm thinking about might have done it, but to roll an armored truck takes experience. Not a bunch of farmhands who run a station every day. And one bloke was killed, another wounded. From what I've seen of them, it just doesn't ring true."

"I've seen a lot of those type of people," Linda said to me. "The ones you'd think that weren't the capable type. Humans continue to surprise me. What are the police doing?"

"I have no idea what they're up to after they found the burnt-out SUV. That's why I need to get back. I'll leave tomorrow."

"What are you going to do about Salvador Franchi?"

"He gave me an ultimatum. Either I look for them and get paid to do it, or he sends his people and creates a mess."

"Do you think you can find them?"

I nodded. "I have a hunch they're there somewhere. If they are, I'll find them."

"And if you do?" Linda asked.

"They'll be dead."

"You're that certain?"

"Yes."

"I'm glad Nicole and the baby are out of the picture."

"All because of a cooler and a missing bull. It sure is fucked up."

Linda said, "I'm sure you're aware of the saying that what seems to be the most obvious isn't always the case?"

"It's bitten me more than once."

She looked at me thoughtfully, her lawyer brain

cycling. "Tell me this. Your friend, Bomber Hansen, how long has he been back in town?"

"Since he got out. Six months."

"Now remember the saying, Mark. If I was you, I'd be keeping one eye in his direction."

Again, she was making sense. "You know, you and Nicole are a lot alike."

She smiled. "The only thing we differ in is our taste in men."

"Really?"

"Yes, I don't like them."

I spent another hour with Nicole before leaving. There was no change to speak of, but her Neuro doctor was positive. Like the rest, he said it was just a matter of time. She was stable, the baby was developing, and the heartbeat was fast and strong.

On returning to the hotel Bomber was missing. Not surprising now that I was considering him in a different light. I called his cell. "Where are you?"

"Out."

I could hear the noise in the background. Music and voices. "The Pink Palace?"

"Maybe."

"Just make sure you're back to leave in the morning. I'm about to book flights."

"Don't wait up," he grunted and disconnected.

I went out onto the balcony and looked at the light-speckled scene before me. Then I looked at the balcony beside me, partitioned by a rendered concrete wall.

There must be a reason.

My phone buzzed. It was Linda. "Hey, has there been a change?"

"No, sorry."

"Okay."

"I asked around a little about your friend, Hansen."

"And?"

"He got out of jail in Dubbo a month before he arrived in Friar's Lake," she explained. "He spent that month in Sydney."

"With his old crew?" I asked.

"Yes. But he wasn't popular with them because when he went to jail, he cost them a fortune in product."

"He seems friendly enough with them at the minute," I said.

"Remember what I said, Mark? He has to be out there for a reason."

"His missus and kid," I theorized.

"Maybe, or maybe it's a good cover for what he's really up to."

"What would that be?"

"That's for you to find out," she replied. "But I'm thinking he was sent out there as a punishment and to redeem himself in the eyes of the Taipans."

This is all I need. "I hope you're wrong, Linda."

"So do I, Mark. I have to go. Be careful."

"Thanks."

How the hell can you be careful twenty floors up and trying to get onto the balcony next door? I swung my leg over the rail and prepared to follow it with the other. I looked down. Not advisable when you're so high. It gave me pause for thought but I still wanted to know if Bomber was hiding something.

Over it went and the way I was situated I was facing back towards the balcony. I edged along it, using the rail for support. All good, unless the railing gave way and I plummeted headfirst to my death. Not a happy thought.

I reached the partition and moved my right arm

around it to grasp the rail on the other side. My feet danced along the narrow edge like a tap dancer, except mine were not choreographed, rather more a case of nerves.

The partition came out about half a foot, to provide privacy for those next door. As I moved around it, I slipped, just lost my footing, and found myself hanging from the rail by one arm, twenty floors up. Not ideal.

I gasped as pain shot through my shoulder, but my grip held firm like a vise. Sweat came immediately to my brow as more than a hint of fear coursed through my veins. I swung my left arm up to grab the rail. My fingers locked around the curved surface, and I grunted as I pulled myself up.

Once my footing was reasonably firm, I paused, taking deep breaths to try and bring my heart rate down, which was threatening to erupt from my chest.

I climbed over the rail and lurched towards the sliding glass door. It was unlocked so I let myself in. Turning on a lamp beside the sofa, it threw enough illumination for me to see my way around.

I looked throughout the suite but found nothing laying around. Then I went into Bomber's bedroom and found his bag. I undid the zipper and started looking through. Nothing. I'd risked my life to get in there, almost died, all for naught.

I left the bedroom and closed the door behind me. Now, back into the main room I stood in the middle and ran my gaze over everything, looking at nothing in particular.

My head stopped, my eyes focusing on the lamp I'd turned on. Whoever had done it was an amateur. I mean, it was affixed to the inside of the lamp shade and casting a small shadow. I walked over and looked inside, seeing the bug.

Now I looked around once more with a renewed vigor. I found two more. One in the room phone, of course there's always one there, just watch the movies. And another under the occasional table.

I took a photo of one of them and put my phone back in my pocket. It was time to leave. I turned off the lamp, and turned towards the door, deciding that risking my life twice wasn't worth it and that I could just lock the door behind me and walk to my own room. But what if someone saw me leaving the room? What if Bomber was in the hallway right now and caught me coming out of his room? Shaking my head, I went back out onto the balcony, and retraced my dangerous steps to my own balcony next door.

Knowing what I knew, I did the same to my room. Guess what? Three bugs in there as well. The question was, what was I going to do about it? After careful consideration for several moments, my decision was made. I said, "Tell Walsh I want to speak to him. Tell him to be here in thirty minutes."

Walsh and Jackson arrived in thirty-five. I let them both in and said, "Weren't that close, I gather."

"What do you want, Hayes?"

"What's with bugging my fucking room?" I asked and dumped the electronic devices into a glass of water.

"Seemed like the thing to do," Walsh replied.

"Really?"

He shrugged. "Well, you're here with a POI and you're seeing another POI. Work it the hell out."

He was getting angry, but I didn't give a shit. "Where is he?"

"Who?"

"Higgins."

He stared at me momentarily then put his hand in his pocket, taking out his cell. He dialed a number and said, "He wants to talk to you."

After a few moments listening, Walsh held out his phone. I shook my head. "No, in person."

The detective inspector put the cell back up to his ear. "Did you get that?"

More listening and then the disconnection. Walsh stared at me. "He'll be here shortly."

It took twenty minutes. Twenty minutes of me staring at the two pricks opposite me. Walsh wasn't that bad, but Jackson was a complete knob.

Higgins was wearing a suit and tie. He looked to be a little grayer than our last encounter Pressure of the job, I guessed. He looked put out. "Mister Hayes."

"Higgins."

"What is it that you want?"

"Are you running this shit show?" I asked him, staring at the two detectives across from me. "Shouldn't you be investigating your own, not the public?"

"That depends."

"Depends?"

"That is right."

"Well, what the bloody hell are you bugging me for?"

"Because you are involved," Higgins said simply.

"Fuck off."

He sighed. "All right let's start with this: last night you were at the Pink Palace. You put two of the Taipans out of action. One will probably never walk right again. Then you are seen with Salvador Franchi, twice. The second time after you were told to stay away. Again, involved. The way I see it, you're interfering with an ongoing investigation. I could have you locked up right now for that alone."

At that point I thought of a great comeback to the threat. "Screw you."

"I'm sure I can think of other reasons to lock you up unless you level with me and—what the hell, I was hoping never to see you ever again. Yet here we are. What the hell are you involved in, Hayes?"

So, it had come down to threats. "Too much. What do you want me to do?"

"There's something going on out there in that shit-hole, Hayes, and I want to know what it is."

"Then go and find out."

"I arrive in town with a task force, and I get nowhere. You, on the other hand, are family. They'll talk to you."

"Now you're pissing up the wrong tree," I scoffed at him.

"I don't think so. Tell me why you've been meeting Salvador Franchi."

"I wanted to know where his two thugs were. The ones I thought shot Nicole."

Higgins nodded. "What did you find out?"

"They're missing. He hasn't heard from them in around two weeks."

"They went to ground after shit blew up and they shot a copper," Higgins suggested.

I shook my head. "He said they went missing before Nicole was shot."

"You believe him?" Walsh asked skeptically. It was the first time he'd spoken in a while.

"He paid me ten grand up front to find them, so yeah, I do believe him."

Higgins stared at me for a minute and then said, "Shit just finds you, doesn't it?"

"It would seem so."

"We're part of a new task force that has been formed

to take down organized crime, Hayes. I'm in charge. You found the girls, find out what's going on."

"You want to tell me what I'm looking for?"

"Let's see. You've got two missing men from the Franchi organized crime syndicate, a former Taipan sergeant-at-arms living there when there is no real reason to. Also—"

"Wait, Hansen has a wife and kid there."

"A wife and kid he separated from a year before he went to prison."

He's out there for a reason.

"Okay."

"Also, there is the stolen money shipment. Any thoughts about that?"

"No idea," I lied.

"It has to be professional, and like I said, people are more likely to talk to you than the police."

I stared at Higgins. "Are you people going to do anything?"

"I will shift a small team to Dubbo. You'll report to whoever I put in charge. By phone, of course. Work fast, Hayes, I don't have a limitless budget."

"And what if I just say no?"

"Then I will arrest you right here, right now. Make your choice."

"Do I get paid?"

Higgins nodded. "The going rate plus expenses. What do you say?"

"Looks like you just hired a private investigator."

CHAPTER ELEVEN

I arrived back in Friar's Lake late the following day on my own. I had no idea where Bomber Hansen was, and for the most part, I was relieved. Before I left, Higgins reached out and gave me the number of the contact I was to use in Dubbo. A detective sergeant named Greg Bryce.

Now, I had to get back to work and find out what Higgins wanted to know.

I grabbed a pad and started writing:

- Missing heavies disappeared before Nic was shot.
- Most likely dead. Who shot them??
- Tom Mason debt paid back. How??
- Did they rob the truck?? No, professional job.
- Boot print at the SUV, Desert Tracks. Local?? See the owner.
- What is Bomber Hansen up to??

The list wasn't long, but it was complex with the possibility of growing branches like a tree.

I fired up Nicole's computer and searched for Stan

Collier. It gave me an address out at Hampton so I decided I would head out there and have a chat the following day.

The next search I did was on Bomber Hansen. What I got was pages of newspaper headlines about him, his arrest, and the trial where he was convicted. From the looks of it, he'd been picked up with others from the Taipans, but he had been the only one convicted. There was no mention of the rest.

I grabbed my phone and punched in the number I had memorized. It rang twice, before, "Bryce."

"It's Mark Hayes."

"What can I do for you, Hayes?" he asked. No introduction, just down to business.

"Why was Bomber Hansen the only one who was convicted and sentenced on his drug bust?"

"He confessed."

"Yes, but what about the others?" I asked.

"He cut a deal, letting them go and he would go down for it all."

I frowned. "Three years doesn't seem much for what he was caught with."

"It doesn't, does it?"

"Who arrested him?"

There was a moment of silence while Bryce went through his mental files. "If I remember rightly, it was Cox and Curtis."

That's right, the coppers at the airport. "Were they the ones who pushed for the deal?"

"I don't know, maybe."

"Can you get me the file?" I asked.

"What for?"

"I want to look at it. Give me some background. Three years isn't much when it comes down to the quantity of drugs and what he was doing with it."

"Are you saying Cox and Curtis are bent, Hayes?"

"No, I'm asking to look at the file."

"I'll see what I can do. Anything else?"

"Yes, nice to meet you."

"Whatever."

The call disconnected.

I stared at the computer screen for another hour before I started going to sleep in front of it. I shut it down and had a shower, before climbing into bed. Tomorrow was another day, and I needed the sleep.

What I would get of it.

Thunder and lightning woke me around three in the morning. There was, however, no lightning in a technical sense; only the thunder of motorcycle engines being revved up. The lightning was their headlights dancing across the wall through the window as they did donuts in the street outside. Then there was the shouting and yahooing.

I scrambled out of bed and grabbed the Glock off the nightstand. I pulled back the curtain marginally so I could see outside and saw four bikers having fun. But it wasn't fun; this was a warning for me. I didn't have to be a genius to work that out.

I had no idea who they were but a fair idea where they came from and who'd put them up to it. Bomber Hansen was sending me a message. What I had to do now was figure out if he knew I was working for the cops or was he warning me away from something totally different.

A few more donuts and they were gone.

When I went outside the following morning to leave, I found Jace and Murphy waiting for me. Jace indicated the black marks on the street and said, "Visitors last night?"

"More like early this morning," I replied.

I had the Glock tucked down the back of my pants, so I was feeling a little on edge.

"Any idea who they were?" Murphy asked.

I glanced at her. "No."

"No, or you're just not saying?"

I smiled at Jace. "Nic's been teaching her a thing or two, huh?"

"Answer the question, Mark."

"Already did."

"When did you get back?"

"Last night."

"Hansen come back with you?"

Word travels. "No, I was on my own. What's with all the questions?"

"Just trying to find out what and why," Jace replied.

"Did something happen while I was away?"

"We're under instruction not to talk to you about anything to do with the case."

"You have any luck with the stolen SUV?" I asked.

"No comment."

"The boot print?"

"No comment."

"Anything?"

"No comment."

"Then fuck off."

They stared at me for a moment before Jace said, "Come on, Jess. I think we've outstayed our welcome."

I watched them drive away and was about to climb into the Monaro when the resident vulture arrived.

Timmins got out of his car and indicated the black marks on the street. "Someone is up for a big tire bill."

"What do you want, Timmins?"

"I heard you had some visitors last night and I was wondering if you could answer a few questions?"

"No."

"Were they bikers?"

"No, they rode frigging kangaroos."

"Were they Taipans?" he persisted.

"What makes you say that?" I asked.

"Whispers are that there's drugs starting to circulate in town again. Now we've got bikers. Do the math and see if you come up with the answer I do."

Now he had my attention. "What drugs?"

"Ice."

"Tell me what you know."

"Quid pro quo. Tell me what you know," he shot back at me.

"Yes, last night they were bikers."

"What ones?" Timmins asked.

I shook my head. "I don't know for sure. Tell me about the drugs."

"Just whispers," he said to me. "People I talk to say there's someone in town selling small bags of Ice."

"Who?"

"They didn't say."

"Who is your informant?" I asked.

He smiled wryly at me. "You don't think I'm going to tell you that, do you?"

"Damn it, Timmins."

"If you answer my next question then maybe I'll think about giving you a name," he said.

"What question?"

"I have a source that tells me a copper here in Friar's Lake is being investigated for corruption."

This was news to me. "Who?"

"Don't you know?"

"The first I've heard about it."

"Shit, I was hoping you'd know." He looked disappointed.

I filed the information. "Who is your informant about the drugs?"

Timmins shook his head. "I said if you answered the question, Mark."

My anger was rising. "How about this? If I find out anything concrete, I'll give you an exclusive."

He snorted. "Yeah, right."

"Listen, Timmins, if this is as big as I think it is, then the press will be crawling all over it and you'll be left out in the cold."

He looked uncertain. His head bobbed almost reluctantly. "All right, but you didn't hear this from me."

"Fine."

"Johnny Moron."

I tried not to laugh. "Where do I find him?"

"He hangs out at the BMX track."

"Old, young—what does he look like?"

"Take me with you and I'll point him out. But I stay in the car."

Sounded all right to me. I'd just put my drive out to Hampton on hold for the moment. What I should have done was phone to find out who the copper they were investigating was. It would have saved me a surprise later on. "Let's go."

"That's him, the bloke in the white tank top and the baseball cap," Timmins said.

"The flighty looking one?"

"Yes."

I reached into the glove compartment and took out an envelope with money in it. I retrieved a hundred-dollar bill and said, "Don't go anywhere."

I worked my way around inconspicuously towards where Moron—shit, someone hated that kid—was standing. I came up behind him and asked, "You Moron?"

It sounded as though I was calling him one. He turned, gave me one glance, and then ran.

I did not need this shit.

So, I followed him, in the Monaro. There was no way I was going to chase the shithead on foot. He ran one way, and I ran towards my car.

"What did you do?" Timmins asked perplexed.

"Not a damn thing," I shot back at him, turning the key in the ignition.

The motor roared to life, and I engaged it into drive. I floored the gas pedal and wheels spun as it shot forward.

"What are you doing?"

"I'm going to run him down."

"What?" Timmins screeched.

"Just shut up and let me drive," I snapped.

I saw Moron disappearing down an alley up ahead, but before I reached it, I turned right into the street before and jumped on the gas. The rear of the Monaro skipped out before snapping back. It flew along the street to the next intersection where I turned left just in time to see the punk emerge from the alley.

"The little prick is quick."

He bolted across the street and jumped a fence. I ripped the handbrake on and spun the steering wheel. When the slide was complete, I let the brake off and the nose of the Monaro was pointed down the alley which ran across the street and kept going.

Once more the beast roared and shot forward as though a lion hunting its prey.

Beside me in the passenger seat Timmins grabbed at the dash and the door handle to steady himself. The car bucked as it crossed the drain at the edge of the street and kept going along the alley. I dodged a couple of large potholes almost deep enough to resemble shell craters.

I glanced right to see if I could see Moron. At first there was nothing but then I caught a glimpse of him hurdling a fence. The pedal went down further.

"Will you slow down?" Timmins yelped.

"You can get out if you want," I flung back at him.

Suddenly I trod on the brakes and the nose of the car lowered as it skidded to a halt. The motor idled as I looked out the window to my right.

"What's wrong?" Timmins asked me.

"Wait."

I couldn't see Moron and was starting to think I had lost him. Then I caught a flash of clothing. I slammed the Monaro into reverse and gave it everything. It shot backward causing Timmins to yelp. "Are you crazy?"

"Just hang on."

The Monaro flew out of the alley onto the street. There was no sign of Moron. My head pivoted as I looked for him. I could feel my anger rising. I needed to question him and couldn't afford to let him get away.

A flash of color told me I had him. Engaged gear, gave the beast gas, and then—BANG!

"What did you do?" Timmins bleated.

I put the Monaro in park and climbed out, walking around to the front of the vehicle. I leaned down and grabbed Moron by the hair. Lifting him up I could see that he had a few scrapes but nothing severe. Being hit by a Monaro would do that to you.

"Hey, what are you doing, man?" he howled as I shoved him into the rear seat.

"Just shut up. I need to talk to you," I snapped.

"You run me down."

"Be thankful I didn't keep going."

I climbed behind the wheel and drove towards the edge of town where I knew there to be a truck stop. From the back I heard Moron say, "Timmins, you bloody snitch. Are you behind this?"

"What are you doing, Mark?" the journo whined. "You hit him with your car."

"He shouldn't have run. I hate running."

"But you didn't run."

"I ran to my car, that was enough."

Two minutes later, I pulled into the truck stop and cut the motor. I turned, digging into my pocket. I held up the hundred and said, "I'm going to ask you some questions. If you can answer them, I'll give you the hundred."

He looked greedily at the money. "What questions?"

"Like who's selling drugs in town?"

He shook his head. "No, I ain't no snitch."

"Who's bringing them in?"

"I don't know."

"Are you sure?"

"Sure, I'm sure. It's just what I've heard."

I put the money back in my pocket. The exercise had been a waste of time.

"Hey, what about the money?" Moron gasped.

"You didn't tell me anything."

"I can find out," he said.

"Find out what?"

"Find out who is bringing them in."

"Sure, you can," I said skeptically.

"Just give me a day or two and I'll have a name for you."

I glanced at Timmins who looked as though he wanted to say something but held it back. I nodded and passed over the hundred for incentive. "Get me a name and I'll give you another."

"Damn right I will," Moron said and climbed out of the rear seat.

"Just be careful, these people won't play nice."

Suddenly he looked confident. "Careful is my middle name."

I watched him run off and turned my attention back to Timmins. "What?"

"I hope you know what you're doing."

"He'll be fine."

CHAPTER TWELVE

I drove out to Hampton with the intent of questioning Stan Collier. He lived in a rundown house with holes in the exterior fiber-cement walls and overgrown garden. Both looked as though they hadn't received any attention for years.

I parked out the front next to a beat-up Holden ute, climbed out of the Monaro, and walked towards the pedestrian gate which hung by one hinge.

The footpath leading to the front door rose and fell as though it had been tortured by an earthquake. Large cracks were punctuated by clumps of dead grass.

I knocked on the door and was greeted by, "What do you want?"

"Stan Collier?" I called back through the closed door.

"Piss off."

"My name is Mark Hayes. I would like to ask you a couple of questions."

No answer.

"I'll make it worth your while."

More silence, and I was about to say more when the door opened and a man with unkempt hair, tattoos, and wearing a stained white T-shirt and holey jeans appeared. "How much?"

"Hundred."

"Wanker," he muttered and started to close the door.

"Two-hundred."

The door stopped. "What do you want to know?"

I was already starting to build a mental file on Collier, and comparing him with the SUV used in the shooting, things didn't stack up. "I wanted to ask you about your stolen SUV, the one which was used in the shooting in Friar's Lake."

"Oh, yeah?" His eyes were suddenly alert. "I already told the cops what I know. It was stolen from right there —" he pointed to the driveway, "out from under my bloody nose."

"When?"

"About two weeks ago."

"About?"

"It's a bit foggy."

I nodded. Drugs or booze, take your pick. "Who owns the ute?"

"It's mine."

"So you own two vehicles?"

"Sure do."

The hell you do, I thought to myself. I would buy that he owned the ute, but not the SUV. "Do you have papers for the SUV?"

"They were in the glove compartment of the vehicle when it was stolen." Rehearsed. "I guess they were burned when whoever torched it."

"Did any of your neighbors see anything?"

"What neighbors?" he asked. "Don't have any."

I nodded. I was forgetting the state of Hampton. It was a small community in its death throes with stuff all to keep it alive. "You kept it in the drive?"

"Yeah."

I reached into my pocket and took out two hundred. I passed it over and said, "Thanks for your time."

As I turned away, I looked down at his feet hoping he would be wearing footwear. I was disappointed to see ten toes, all in need of a farrier. The door closed behind me. Upon hearing it, I changed direction to walk out the opening of the driveway. There was no concrete here, just dirt. I looked at the tire marks in the deep ruts, formed by a vehicle driving in when the dirt had been turned to mud.

Then I compared them to the ute parked outside and came to the conclusion that I needed to add Stan Collier to my ever-growing list. He was a liar.

On the drive back to Friar's Lake I mulled over a few things in my head. Stan Collier had lied to me, and I suspected was never the owner of the SUV. Drugs were being shipped into Friar's Lake once more, and an officer of the law was being investigated for corruption. Then there were the bikers. They were more than likely responsible for the drugs coming in, but how were they doing it. Bomber Hansen? Maybe.

That didn't tell me who shot the shit out of Nicole's home and almost killed her. But there was still the boot print. It was about the only lead I had at this point. Then the thought came to me. Tom Mason. I needed to talk to him.

I didn't get very far before Rob Haskins and Detective Sergeant Naomi Such pulled me over on the way out of town.

I turned off the motor and rolled down my window, the flashing lights on the police 4X4 bouncing off the rearview mirror into my eyes. "Did I forget to indicate at the last turn?"

"Can you step out of the vehicle, Mister Hayes?" Such asked, her tone firm.

I glanced at Haskins who rested his right hand on the butt of his police-issue sidearm. Shit was serious.

"What's going on?" I asked Such.

"Just get out of the vehicle."

"All right." I climbed out and stood with my arms folded across my chest.

"Turn and face the car, hands behind your head."

"You're shitting me?"

"Do it," Haskins snapped.

There is a time for being a smartass and a time for not; this was one of the latter. I complied with the directive and minutes later I found myself mirandized, cuffed, and riding in the back of a police vehicle back to the Friar's Lake station.

"Do you want a lawyer?" Such asked me.

"Do I need one? You still haven't told me what this is about."

"All in good time," Waters replied.

It wasn't the first time I had been in an interrogation room, probably wouldn't be my last, but before I played the ace up my sleeve, I wanted to find out what the hell this was all about. "Are you going to ask me a question or what?"

"Tell us about the evening Sergeant Nicole Berger was shot," Such said.

"I already did."

"Do it again."

So I did.

"You had never seen the vehicle in question before?"

"No."

"Had Sergeant Berger?"

"How should I know?"

"Has everything been all right at home?"

I frowned. "Fine."

"No money problems?"

Now alarm bells were going off. "What do you mean?"

"Money," said Waters. "You know, the stuff you spend, buy things with?"

"I know what money is, you fuckwit."

"Watch your mouth," Such cautioned me.

"Then how about you stop frigging around and get to the point, Sergeant Schultz." My patience was gone.

Such opened a folder she'd brought into the room with her and took out a sheet of paper. She slid it across the table, placing it in front of me. It only took a glance to see what I was looking at. It was a bank statement. As my eyes ran down the page, they stopped at the line saying there had been a credit placed into her account for $50,000. The date on it was the day she had been shot.

"Maybe your partner was the target after all," Such said.

"This is bullshit."

"Do you know where the money came from, Mark?"

So, it was Mark now. Get all friendly in the hope I'll open up. "No, I don't. Do you?"

"We'll find out."

However, she wasn't done there. Another item slid across the table. This time it was a photo. In it was me, Nicole, and Bomber Hansen. It had been taken from across the street the day we were outside the café when I'd caught Tommy Hansen stealing.

"What's this about?"

"Where did you get that?" I snapped.

"Not for you to worry about," Waters said. "Answer the question."

"It was nothing."

"You're both talking to a known felon," Such pointed out. "Were you arranging for the payment to be put into your bank?"

"No. Screw you."

She grinned at me. "Raw nerve?"

"I caught his kid stealing. He came to talk about it."

"Where from?"

"The café where we were. The owner will back the story."

"I guess we'll be talking to her then. Now, let's get back to the money."

"Phone call."

"What?"

"I want to make a phone call."

"Are you saying you want a lawyer?" Such asked.

I shook my head. "No, I'm saying I want to make a bloody phone call. Are your ears painted on?"

"I don't like your tone, Hayes," Such scolded me.

"And I don't like your bullshit. Phone, now."

She took me out into the hall and stood off to one side while I made the call. I skipped the middleman and went straight to the top.

"Hello?" Higgins said.

"You could have given me a bloody head's up, you wanker," I snarled quietly. Well, as quietly as I could as trembling hands held the receiver.

"Nice to talk to you, too, Hayes. Now, tell me what the problem is that you couldn't use your contact."

I gave him the short version of my predicament.

"And is she bent, Hayes?" he asked calmly.

"Screw you. Get me out of here. I can't do what you want if I'm cooped up in here."

"Sit tight. I'll have you sprung in a few hours."

"You can't do it over the phone?" I asked incredulously.

"Just don't answer any more questions."

"Did you know?" I asked him.

"Something did come across my desk," Higgins admitted.

"And you never thought to tell me?"

"Listen, Hayes, I've seen her record and I don't believe it for a second. But, if you want to clear her name, then find out what is going on."

The call disconnected and I hung the phone up. I looked at Such. She gave me a cocky smile and asked, "Done?"

"Yeah."

I was taken back to the interrogation room where I was questioned some more. And as I was advised, I said nothing. Five hours later, after the sun had gone down, a knock came to the interview room door and a detective wearing a suit entered. He carried a piece of paper and said, "I'm Detective Sergeant Greg Bryce. This interview is over."

Well, you would have thought someone had just stolen the two detectives' bag of sweets as they tried to comprehend what had just happened.

"Get up, Hayes, you're leaving," Bryce said.

"Wait just a bloody minute," Such growled. "On whose authority is this happening?"

Bryce handed her the sheet of paper. "This should be enough."

By the time she had finished reading, we were gone.

Once we were outside the station, Bryce said, "I want a beer. Your shout."

He was a middle-aged man with graying hair and stress lines starting to form on his face. But he still looked fit, not letting himself go as the years claimed him. "Seems fair enough. We can talk while we're drinking it."

Ten minutes later, we were in the pub, and I was ordering two beers from the new publican, Rex Folds. "Carlton Draught, Mark?" he asked.

"Yes, Rex, that'll do."

He brought back the bottles and after paying for them, we found a vacant table away from the others and sat down. "You want to tell me what's going on?" I said to Bryce.

He took a pull of his beer. "Not much to tell at the moment. The others on the team in Dubbo are working on it. Although it doesn't look great when that amount of money shows up in a copper's bank account."

"Yeah, well in spite of what they're thinking, she's not bent," I growled.

"We don't think that either, but we have to let it play out until we know what is going on. What about you? Do you have anything yet?"

"Bikers and drugs," I said.

"Come again?"

"There are bikers in town who seem to not like me, and someone is bringing drugs into the town." I told him about the bikes outside Nicole's place and how I was working with an informant trying to find out who was responsible for the drugs.

Bryce said, "In my experience, one generally goes hand in hand with the other."

"If they're Taipans, I agree."

"Watch your ass. Anything else?"

"I went and talked to Stan Collier out at Hampton

today. He's the bloke who supposedly owned the SUV that was involved in the shooting."

"And?"

"He never owned it," I replied. "He says he did, but he's lying. I need to do some background on him."

"I'll have my people take care of it," Bryce said. "I'll phone you the results. Shouldn't take more than twenty-four hours. Any progress on the Franchi thing?"

"No, haven't got that far yet. I was going to see a POI about it today, but I got tied up."

Bryce gave a wry grin. "Yeah. Do you carry?"

"A Glock."

"Registered?"

"Category H."

He looked at me skeptically. "Is there anything else you need?"

"Not yet," I replied. "If you can get me the information about Collier that would be great."

"Consider it done."

"Thanks."

Who would have thought a missing cooler and bull would have led to this? I had reminiscences of the Ten Cent case, only this was much more dangerous.

The next morning, I walked out into the steamy early morning heat to find Jace waiting for me. He was leaning against the Monaro at the edge of a puddle filled by a late-night storm. I had been so tired, I barely remember the booming rattling the windows. "You take lessons from Tom?" I asked him, referring to the previous sergeant, Tomika Rains. Sadly, she'd been shot and died in my arms.

"She was a good boss," he replied.

I nodded. "What can I do for you, Jace?"

"I want to know what's going on," he said.

"With what?"

"You get dragged into the station and hours later a detective comes along and gets you out. I know Nic isn't dirty, Mark, but if I'm to help, I need to know what's happening."

"Let it go, Jace," I said to him. "If I need help, I'll reach out. Just leave it."

"Are you in trouble, Mark?"

I shook my head. "What have they found out about the armored truck heist?"

"Not much. Whatever they know they're not telling. They've not even found the prime mover that was used."

"A lot of places to hide it, I guess," I replied.

"Maybe."

"Anything on the blokes who shot at the house?"

Jace shrugged. "I think they figure if they solve the issue with the money and Nic the rest will resolve itself. Oh, I almost forgot. Robbery and the Serious Crimes Squad are sending a task force out here to take over the heist case."

"Thanks, Jace."

"Just let me know if I can help."

"No worries."

I went to the Western Plains Heritage Bank to see the manager, Bill Walker. I needed to get answers about the money in Nicole's account. I waited twenty minutes to see him.

He called me into his office and showed me a chair. I sat and looked around. The interior of his office, like the rest of the bank, was period decorated.

"It's good to see you, Mark," Walker said to me. "How is Nicole getting on?"

"Still the same."

"I'm sorry to hear that. What can I do for you?"

"While Nicole is laid up, I'm stuck with doing everything else. Banking and such so she doesn't get everything repossessed. I—"

He held up his hands. "Mark, I can't get you any money out of Nicole's account. I hope you're not going to ask me about that."

I shook my head. "No, not at all. I've got all that sorted. But I noticed a rather large payment has gone into her account, and I was concerned that there might have been a bank error. You know what the banks are like when it comes to money."

He frowned. "Oh, dear, let's have a look. When did it go in?"

"Let's see, ah, the fifteenth of this month."

His fingers skipped across the keys and his facial expression changed when he found what I was talking about. "Oh, yes, there it is. You're right, that's quite a sum."

"Is it a bank error?"

Walker tapped some keys, clicked the mouse, and said, "It doesn't look to be."

"Are you sure?"

"Yes."

"Can you tell me where it came from? I would like to call them and make sure before any nasty letters start arriving in the mail."

"I'm not sure I should—"

My cell started to buzz in my pocket, but I ignored it. "Don't be worried about me stealing the money, Bill. If I wanted to do that I would have already. I just want to head off potential trouble before it starts."

"Well—all right. Let's see, the company name is called, Wyatt Holdings PTY LTD."

I stood up and held out a hand. "Thanks, Bill. You've saved me a headache."

"Pleased to be of service, Mark."

By this time, the cell in my pocket had stopped buzzing like an angry bee, however, once I got back outside, it started again. The number was blocked but I had an idea who it was. I was about to answer it when a shadow appeared in front of me.

"Hey, Mark, how's things?"

My blood ran cold for standing in front of me was Bomber Hansen. "Hi, Bomber, what's up?"

"Not much, just saw you come out of the bank and thought I'd come and check out how that pretty copper of yours is getting on."

"Fine, Bomber, just fine. How's your kid, staying out of trouble?"

"Yeah, the little prick."

We stared at each other for a moment, and I figured it was his way of letting me know that he was back in town. I said, "Anyway, I've got to go. Be seeing you around."

"Yeah, sure."

I climbed into the Monaro and used my mirrors to track Bomber's movements. He crossed the dusty street and got into the passenger side of a Ford Ranger 4X4.

Not all bikers ride bikes all the time.

My cell buzzed again, and I answered. It was Bryce.

CHAPTER THIRTEEN

"We found out some interesting things about Stan Collier," he said to me.

"I'm listening."

"The guy got out of Dubbo Jail around six months ago. He was in for drug possession and assault police."

"Would the detectives investigating the shooting know this?" I asked.

"I can't answer that. I don't know."

"So, he could be involved with the shooting?"

"I don't think so. He's not the type. No firearms charges on his rap sheet. But he might know who was. He's just a piece of a larger puzzle. But he did share a cell at one time with your mate, Hansen."

"Which means all roads lead to Bomber Hansen," I replied.

"Yes, but what does he have against you?"

"Nothing that I know of. We never really crossed paths until recently."

"Then figure it out, Hayes, before you wind up dead and buried in a forty-four-gallon drum."

"I'll work on it. I have something for you. The money that went into Nicole's account is from a company called Wyatt Holdings PTY LTD."

"I'll have my team look into it. How did you get that?"

"I'm resourceful."

"Right."

With the call done I thought for a moment. Collier had links to Bomber Hansen, and I had a line on where the money came from. None of it got me closer to Franchi.

Desert Tracks boots.

Collier had links to Hansen. Collier never really owned the SUV. Desert Tracks boot print where the SUV was burnt out—Tom Mason and Jimmy Morrison needed half a million dollars. They wore Desert Tracks boots. I was missing something.

As it worked out, I didn't have to leave Friar's Lake to see Tom Mason; he was already in town with Betty.

I caught sight of them going into the men's apparel shop. I pulled the Monaro over and climbed out after turning the motor off. Inside, my nose was assaulted by the same smells as in the first visit.

Looking around I saw them over at the section where moleskins and jeans were displayed on racks. I hurried across to them. "Tom Mason, just the person I was looking for. Saved me a trip going out to your place."

He gave me a wary look before saying, "What do you want, Hayes?"

"I need to have a talk to you about some money. We can do it here or somewhere a little more private. Your choice."

"Why don't you leave us alone?" Betty sneered at me.

Well, I guess I wasn't the flavor of the month anymore. I suppose she was getting enough of it from Tom. "I will, once I get answers to my questions."

"What do you want to know?" Tom asked in a hushed voice.

"I had an enlightening conversation with Salvador Franchi when I was in Sydney. Do you know what he said to me? He said you paid your debt in full. Now, I'm curious. Where did you get the money?"

He glared at me. "None of your damn business."

"Five-hundred grand. That's a lot of money to come up with, especially when you didn't have it. Robbed any armored trucks lately?"

"What?"

"You heard."

"Just fuck off and leave us alone," Betty hissed.

"I'm still waiting for an answer to my question, Tom. Want to prove me wrong?"

"Damn right you're wrong. The old man sold some land. We got enough money to pay the debt off."

"You mean you told your father about your debt, and he sold land to pay it off?"

"That's right."

I stared at him to see if he was lying to me or not. He was either telling the truth or he was very good at lying. I wasn't quite sure.

I was about to press him with more questions when my phone buzzed. It was starting to become a very busy morning. I pressed answer.

"Hello, Mark Hayes speaking."

"Mark, it's Grandma Mary. I need your help."

Grandma Mary was an Aboriginal woman who lived out at Hampton. She had played a pivotal role in helping me solve the Ten Cent killings. I would have dismissed the call except she was whispering, and it sounded important. "What's wrong, Mary?"

"Some local boys, they found a car."

"All right. So what's important about this car?"

"It has dead men in it, Mark. Two of them."

I froze. A million things started running through my mind. "What color, Mary?"

"It's blue."

"I'll be there soon."

I disconnected the call and looked at Tom Mason. "I have to go. But I'll be back to ask you more questions."

"Don't bother," Betty growled. "Just stay the hell away from us."

I needed fuel before going out to Hampton, so I stopped at the roadhouse on the highway and filled up the Monaro. I went inside and found Cheryl behind the counter. She was a young Aboriginal woman who'd been working there for the past month. I'd had a few dealings with her, and she seemed quite pleasant and happy.

I paid with a $100 note, and she was making change which included a $20. She was about to hand it over when she noticed that it had a red mark on it. "I'll get you another one. You don't want this one," she said.

I shrugged my shoulders. "Don't worry about it. It'll do, it all spends."

I put the money in my pocket and before I left, I had a thought. "Cheryl, have you seen any bikers getting around town of late? Maybe they've come in to get fuel?"

She looked thoughtful. "Not in the past few days, but there was a couple about a week ago."

"Did they have jackets on?"

"Yes, they did, leather ones."

"Did they have anything on the back of them?" I asked.

She shook her head. "No, I think they were plain."

"Thanks for that."

I should have been in a hurry to get out to Hampton, but I wasn't. If they were dead, they were going nowhere, and I wasn't really looking forward to the sight that was going to greet me. They would have been in the car for days now and the smell would be overwhelming from this heat.

As I climbed into the Monaro and put the key in the ignition, I suddenly realized something. The two bikers in town would have been there just before the armored truck got robbed. This shot them to the top of my list.

It took me 45 minutes to get out to Hampton. Once there I pulled up at Grandma Mary's House and climbed out. She met me at the front door, unchanged from the last time that I had seen her. Iron gray hair still the same.

"How have you been, Mary?"

"The dreams have stopped, Mark. That is something."

The dreams to which she referred were about the girls who came to her at night. The ones that had been murdered and buried in the sinkholes in Friar's Lake. "I'm pleased. Tell me about this car."

She looked over her shoulder and called out, "Lionel, get out here."

A 14-year-old boy appeared behind her. She said, "This is my grandson, Lionel. Him and a few of his mates they found the car. You tell Jim Rockford where you found it."

"Over by Bottle Street."

"Where's that?" I asked.

"You go and show him," Grandma Mary ordered, pushing him out the door in front of her.

"Come on then," Lionel said grudgingly.

He brushed past me down the stairs. I looked up at the old woman. "Thanks, Mary."

"You just keep us out of it. There is enough trouble around here without more."

"What do you mean?" I asked her.

"Just trouble, all right?"

I nodded and followed Lionel out of the yard.

He showed me the way. About two streets across we came to the edge of town where houses had been abandoned. Now they were nothing but trashed shells. Which made the blue BMW Series 4 look out of place.

"Did you touch anything?" I asked Lionel.

"Just the tarp, ay."

He pointed to the messy lump beside the vehicle. The tarp lay beside the BMW. "What made you look?"

"Never seen it before. Looked out of place."

"All right. Go back home to Grandma Mary's. I might need to ask you another question or two later on. Was there anyone else with you?"

"Just Robert."

"Well, tell him not to talk about this with anyone, okay?"

He nodded and walked away.

Two weeks in this heat does things to bodies locked up in vehicles. Nasty things. I cautiously approached the BMW. The smell emanating from within told me that I'd been right about the heat. I didn't bother about opening any doors. I didn't think my stomach could handle it. Peering through the window I could see the swarm of flies within. The sight wasn't pretty. From what I could see I gathered both of the deceased had been shot in the head. How could I tell? They had not been there two weeks.

There were two calls I needed to make.

"Yeah?" Bryce answered on the second ring.

"I found those two thugs."

"Where?"

"Dead in their BMW. Looks like someone took them out."

He grunted. "Doesn't surprise me. Where abouts?"

"Hampton."

"I know where that is."

"What do you want me to do?" I asked.

"Have you let Franchi know, yet?"

"I called you first before I called him."

"Make the call, Hayes. I'll dispatch someone to watch the scene to see what the old man does."

"All right."

"Good work. How did you find them?"

"Doesn't matter. Just luck. Don't you want to investigate it?"

"Not yet. I figure we know who it was," he replied.

"Would you like to tell me?" I asked him.

"Taipans. It adds up. You've got bikers and Franchi family in the same area. Things are bound to come to a head eventually. It just confirms that the Taipans are up to something."

It made sense, I guess. "I'll make the call."

Salvador Franchi took a little longer to answer. When he did, he sounded tired. "You have news, Mister Hayes?"

"Yes. I found your men."

"Are they dead?"

"You could say that."

"Where are they?"

I told him. All of it, how they'd been shot and dumped.

"I will see to it from here. Thank you, Mister Hayes. I'll see that you get the rest of your money."

I suddenly realized that I didn't want it anymore. "Don't worry about it, I didn't do much."

"A deal is a deal. You will get it. There will be extra."

"Extra for what?"

"I want you to find out who killed them."

Then he was gone.

Before leaving, I looked around the area, working in a growing circle as I went. At first, the scene looked clear but then I saw them. Bike tracks. Not ones from local kids, motorcycles.

I took pictures with my cell and left.

Back at Grandma Mary's I knocked on the door again. She answered and asked, "Is it taken care of?"

"It will be. Just keep it under your hat for the time being."

"We're black fellas. No one listens to us around here." She stared at me, remembering. "Almost no one."

"Can you tell me if there have been any bikers around town at all?"

"No."

"Are you sure? Haven't heard anything?"

"No."

"What about Lionel?"

"Lionel!" she called back over her shoulder.

"What now?" The young man sounded far from happy.

"Get out here."

"What do you want?"

When he appeared, she cuffed him up the back of his head. "This fella has another question for you."

"What?"

"Have you seen any bikers around town?"

Lionel frowned. "Not seen, heard one the other day."

"Early? Late?"

"Late in the afternoon."

"How long do you think that car was there?"

"Few days."

I nodded. "Thanks. Take care."

I sat in the Monaro and contemplated my next move. I had been right. The deaths were recent. Done with pussy-footing around, I drove to Collier's place. It was time to get some concrete answers.

"You again!" was all he got out before my fist hit him flush in the face. He fell backward with a grunt and sat down hard on the floor. Then I entered and closed the door behind me.

"What are you doing, man?" he wailed as I grabbed a handful of greasy hair and started dragging him along the hallway to the kitchen.

"Just shut up, you lying piece of shit," I snarled at him.

"Let me go! Let me go!"

We reached the kitchen, and not releasing my grip I lifted him onto a chair beside the kitchen table. His hand scrabbled for a knife and was about to lock around its hilt when I brought my fist down upon it.

Another howl of pain.

My right hand grabbed him around the throat, squeezing fiercely. "Don't move."

His eyes bulged until I let go. He coughed violently while I looked around the kitchen. I found an old kettle with a detachable cord. "That will do."

Within moments, I had it unplugged and then stood

in front of the still-stunned Collier. There was a trickle of blood running from the corner of his mouth. "What do you want?"

"I have some more questions for you. This time I want truthful answers."

"Okay."

"The SUV, where did it come from?"

"I bought it."

The cord suddenly looped around his throat, and I pulled it tight. Within moments his tongue protruded, and he was changing color. He fought wildly against it until I released the tension and let air through. I hit him again. "Tell the truth, Collier."

"It is, I bought it with the money they gave me."

"Who gave you?"

"I don't know."

I stepped forward again.

"Wait!" he screeched. "I'm telling the truth."

"Was it Bomber Hansen?"

"No. I'd never seen them before."

"Were they bikers?"

"No—yes."

"Which is it? No, or yes?"

"Both. They rode bikes but I couldn't see any colors. They weren't patched."

"Could they have been removed?"

"I guess."

"Taipans?"

"No—I don't know."

I glared at him. "Tell me what happened. From the start."

"I moved out here to get away from everything," Collier said. "I knew about this place from Bomber when we were in prison. He'd talked about it, said it was a ghost town. Sounded good to me. Just came out, found a livable place, and moved in. Only needed a bit of power so I bought a generator. Then some guys I'd never seen before knocked on my door. Offered me ten grand if I went out and bought an SUV in my name. Said they would even pay for that."

"Where did you get it?" I asked him.

"That old bloke in Friar's Lake. Cecil?"

"Cyril?"

"Yeah, that's him. They said once I bought it, to let them know and they'd come and get it."

"Is that what happened?"

"Yes. When they picked it up, they would then call me to let me know when to report it stolen."

"Did they ring you on your cell?"

"No, one they gave me."

"Where is it?"

"Burnt in a forty-four in the back yard. They told me to get rid of it."

"What did they look like?" I asked.

"Big blokes. Dark hair, tattoos."

"Have you heard from them since?"

"No."

I nodded. "One last thing. Have you seen Bomber Hansen since you've been back?"

Collier shook his head. "No."

"Any idea how the drugs are getting into Friar's Lake?"

"No."

"Fine."

Then I left.

"Jace."

"Collier lied to you. He was told to report the SUV stolen when a call was made."

"Mark? Is that you?"

"Yes," I replied into my cell. "It was set up for a while before it was executed—"

My brakes came on hard and I pulled off the road under a tall gum tree. It had taken a minute, but my words had suddenly dawned on me. It had all been planned.

"Are you still there, Mark?"

"Yes, did you hear what I said? It was planned ahead of time. I'm thinking that the money into the bank was as well."

"Did Collier tell you this?"

"Yes, it might pay to pick him up before he disappears."

"Shit, Mark, what are you doing?"

"Trying to find out who shot Nicole."

"Mark—"

I hung up on him before he could ask any more questions. As I stared ahead into the shimmering distance, a galah swooped low across the rugged road. I was so occupied with my thoughts that I never noticed the white Toyota 4X4 pull up a short distance behind me.

It wasn't until the occupants opened fire, I found that out.

"Shit! Fuck!" I shouted as glass and bullets sprayed through the rear window. I felt them punch into the car and seat as I hunched down, trying to grab the Glock from the glove compartment.

My shaking hand reached out and touched the lock just as a bullet punched into the dropdown lid. I flinched and swore again, a string of epithets which would have curled a sailor's hair.

I tried again, and this time the lid dropped down revealing my handgun. Meanwhile the shooters kept up their steady rate of fire. I grabbed the Glock and pointed it over my shoulder out of the opening that had once housed the rear window. I fired five shots—maybe six—rapidly, the sound within the Monaro making my ears ring.

Although I didn't see it, the shooters were taken aback by me firing at them. They ducked down behind the trunk and started firing once more.

Risking a bullet, I reached up and turned the rearview mirror downward so I could see out the back. I could see them moving, though not clearly.

I lifted the Glock again and fired once more, four rounds this time.

One of them cried out and stumbled backward. It was then that I noticed they were armed differently than when Nicole was shot. These assholes had rifles, not assault weapons.

I blew off the rest of the magazine and that seemed to do the trick. While I fumbled for a magazine to reload, they backpedaled to their vehicle and jumped inside.

Soon they sped past me and disappeared into the haze while I was searching for that elusive magazine. Shit.

Cyril almost cried when I drove the Monaro into his yard full of bullet holes and mostly windowless. It had once been his pride and joy, and it broke his heart to see the condition it was now in.

"Mark, what did you do?"

"It wasn't me. Some bastards tried to kill me again."

"The same as last time?"

"No, this time it was different."

"Did you report it?" he asked.

"Not yet. Can you fix it?"

Cyril stood beside the beast and scratched his head. "If it is only superficial—"

"It is. The motor is fine."

"It might take a while."

"Have you got something I can use?"

Minutes later, he had me set up with an 80 Series Land Cruiser. "Thanks, Cyril."

"I would appreciate it back in one piece."

"Also, did a guy buy a dark Ford Explorer off you around two weeks ago?"

Cyril frowned. "Maybe. We can check the books."

"Please."

We went inside and in the stifling heat, Cyril looked over his books. "Sorry about the aircon. Packed up the other day and I haven't had it fixed. Cheap piece of shit."

"Why don't you open the windows?" I asked him.

"They're screwed shut. Pricks around here steal." He paused as he ran his finger along a line in a ledger. "Here it is. Yes, I sold a Ford Explorer to a bloke named Collier."

"How did he pay for it?"

"In cash."

"Thanks, Cyril."

"Anytime. I'll let you know when I get started on your Monaro."

That night I rang to see how Nicole was getting on. As usual there was no change, but the specialist wasn't concerned. I got the usual 'This takes time' speech.

Afterwards I checked in with Bryce who told me that a team was onsite surveilling the BMW and that I couldn't have the files on the detectives that I asked for. However, he did have news on the company Wyatt Holdings.

"One of my people traced it to a shell corporation overseas. After that it went nowhere."

"Better than nothing," I replied.

"Yeah, it's something. How are you traveling?"

"There was an incident today."

"What kind of incident?"

I told him what happened. "Shit, Hayes, have you reported it?"

"That's what I'm doing now."

"Are you alright?" he asked before answering himself. "Of course, you are."

I said, "I think I might have hit one of them."

"Pity he didn't stay down. Bikers do you think, or Franchi?"

"I don't know. Never got a good look at them."

"Anything more to report?"

I thought about the question and said, "Something isn't right."

"You're damn straight on that one."

"No, the hit on me was set up ahead of time."

"How do you mean?" Bryce asked.

I told him and then threw the money into the mix. "I think the money in Nicole's account is part of it."

"So, you're saying that you have no idea who is behind it."

"Pretty much."

"Shit. Keep at it. Do you want me to relocate the team?" Bryce asked me, concern in his voice.

"No, I can still be killed either way."

"That's the spirit." The sarcasm was obvious. "Higgins said to tell you you're doing great."

"Tell Higgins to stick it up his ass."

"Will do. Take care."

I lay back on the lounge, feeling a headache coming on. Everything was just a jumble, a big mess that seemed to keep getting bigger. Dead thugs, drugs, people trying to kill me, and bikers. Could it get any frigging worse?

What a stupid question. Of course, it could.

CHAPTER FOURTEEN

It started with a text the next morning. Just a simple two-word message: Bodies gone. Then came the knock at the door. I tucked the Glock in the back of my pants and opened it to find two men wearing jeans and shirts and sunglasses carrying a briefcase. "Mister Franchi sends his regards."

Then they left.

I took the briefcase into the kitchen and placed it on the table and opened it. I almost fell over. At a rough guess there was around thirty thousand in cash staring back at me. On top was a handwritten note. It just said: A Bonus.

Then came a second knock on my door. I never thought, just opened it and found a fist thrust into my guts. "What did they want?" Bomber Hansen snarled at me, forcing me back as I gasped for air.

"Great to see you, too, Bomber," I managed to reply.

He closed the door behind him. "Don't shit me, Hayes. They were Franchi's men, I'd know them anywhere."

"They brought me some money."

"What for?"

"Because I found his two missing men."

"You what?"

"You know what else I found with them?" I asked.

"What?"

"Bike marks."

"So?"

"Are there some of your Taipan biker friends out here, Bomber?"

He glared at me. "Frig off they are."

"Are you sure?"

"Of course, I'm bloody sure."

"Then who were the assholes on bikes doing donuts outside on the street the night before last?"

"How the shitting hell should I know?" Bomber growled.

"And the drugs coming into town. Come on, Bomber, you must know something."

"Screw you."

"You can't tell me you know nothing about it?" I prodded.

"Just because there are drugs in town doesn't mean I'm responsible."

"Then who is?" I snapped at him.

"Probably the same pricks who shot up your house and put your missus in hospital. Maybe the ones who killed those two thugs you were looking for, or the same assholes who killed that Moron kid."

"Whoa, back up."

"What?"

"What about the Moron kid?"

"He was found dead in the park this morning. Someone had stabbed him."

My heart fell and I felt as though Bomber had

punched me in the stomach again. "Are—are you sure it was him?"

Bomber nodded. "Sure, I'm sure. Why?"

"Then it's my fault."

"What the hell are you on about?" he asked.

"I paid him money to get me a name of who was smuggling drugs into Friar's Lake."

"Well, if he found out anything, he isn't going to tell you. He should have been more careful," Bomber stated.

Anger burned deep within me. My hand reached around to my Glock, and I whipped it out, placing it forcefully under Bomber's chin. "If you had anything to do with this, Bomber, I promise you, you won't see the end of the week."

"Wow, easy there, ranger. I promise you I had nothing to do with it. OK? I don't do that shit anymore. I can try to find out though, to prove it wasn't me. Shouldn't cost too much."

"How much?" I was flat, my tone low.

"Give me a couple of grand and I'll get it done."

I shook my head. "You're unbelievable."

"You want these pricks or not?"

"Yes, I do."

"Then give me the money."

Wow, for those of you who are as confused as me, this is what we have in a nutshell. A bloody big nutshell. I was hired to find a cooler and a bull, which led to a bloke getting beat up and dying. Then someone tried to kill me, and it was Nicole who paid that price. I was hired by a mobster to find two missing men. Done that, both dead. Now he wants me to find those responsible. Also, I was nicked as forced labor for a special team within New

South Wales Police to find out what is happening in Friar's Lake. Nicole has been set up for taking a bribe, someone tried to kill me again, drugs are back on the street, and the young bloke I hired to find out who was doing it has been murdered. And let's not forget the bikers and the former sergeant-at-arms for the Taipans Motorcycle Club who I just hired again. To top it all off, I have no idea who is responsible.

Truly, you can't make this shit up.

After Bomber left, I went down to the park. There was a crowd gathered watching the police do their thing. However, when Timmins saw me, he stomped right up to me, put his face in mine, and said, "This is your damn fault."

"Timmins, wait. I—"

"Wait bullshit. If you hadn't have given him money, then he would still be alive."

I shoved him away from me. "Back off."

"Is there a problem here?"

I turned my head to look at Jace. "No, no problem."

"The hell there isn't," Timmins snarled. "You tell him, or I will."

"Tell me what?"

"Moron was helping me with something before this happened," I replied.

"Christ, Mark, wait here."

I watched him walk over to Such who stared at me while he told her what she needed to know. She ceased what she was doing and walked over to where I stood with Timmins. "You got some light to shed on this?"

She wasn't happy; didn't blame her really. "I might."

She held up the police tape. "Follow me."

As we walked away from the rest, Such said, "Tell me."

Suddenly I was aware of the loud buzzing of cicadas

all around me, spurred on by the heat. "There are drugs getting into the town. He knew a little about it. I asked him some questions and gave him some money to find out a name."

"And got him killed." Her voice was cold.

At least she wasn't accusing me of the murder. Yet. "It would seem so."

"What did he tell you, Hayes?"

I related the story to her. Once I was done, there was a drawn-out period of silence. Then she asked me, "Does this have anything to do with that copper who got you out of jail?"

"I can't say."

"I'll take that as a yes. What is going on?"

"I can't say."

"Then I'll lock you up."

"We all know how that went last time."

"Christ, Hayes?"

"You know Collier lied, right?" I asked.

"Yes. I sent two officers out to pick him up this morning."

"It was set up ahead of time, you know that right. Which means the money into Nicole's account was prearranged, too."

"How do you know this?" she asked me, scowling.

"Because I already talked to Collier like you lot should have done in the first place."

"Interfering again."

I looked over where the activity was around the body. "Can I go now?"

Such nodded. "Don't leave town. I'll most likely need to talk to you again."

I called Bryce. "This is bullshit. Tell Higgins I'm out."

"Ease up, China, what has happened?"

"I got someone killed is what happened."

"Who?"

"A young bloke who was trying to find me a name."

"What name?"

"One that puts it to whoever is bringing drugs into town."

"It's not just there you know."

"What?"

"The whole west is alive with Ice at the moment. Someone has expanded their business big time and we need to know who."

Anger flared. "What the hell, Bryce. Is this what it's all about? You have me sniffing around looking for a drug supplier?"

"That's most of it. But there's a little more to it than that."

"Do tell." Sarcasm dripped from my voice.

"We had a UC go in. He was picked up in Dubbo and vanished. We lost contact with him almost immediately."

"Bloody hell. When?"

"A month ago, when it started taking off."

I shook my head. He couldn't see me do it, but I was, and I wasn't happy. "There's more to it, Bryce. I can feel it."

"There is but I can't tell you. Not yet."

"I can tell *you* this. It's not Franchi because he hired me to find out who it was that killed his men and left them to fester. And it's not Bomber Hansen because he is trying to find out who is bringing the drugs in. That means it's a third party. *They* killed Franchi's men posing as bikers, trying to put heat on the Taipans. And they came after me, making me think they were Franchi's men."

"Talk later, Mark."

Anger again. "Shit a frigging brick, Bryce. You know it's a third party. What the hell do you need me for if you already know?"

"We need you to figure out the operation."

"Did you know I was a target? Did Higgins?"

"Take care, Mark."

"Damn it, talk to me."

The line went dead.

Timmins climbed into the Land Cruiser passenger seat. "They should have locked you up."

"Maybe they will after this is over," I replied quietly.

He frowned at me, expecting more. "What is it?"

"I think someone else is mixed up in this."

"How do you mean?"

I shook my head. "The less you know, the better."

"I'd like to help."

I looked into his tired brown eyes. "It could get you killed, Timmins."

"Like it or not, Mark, I'm involved. Remember, I was the one who took you to him. That makes me responsible, too."

"I was talking to a source inside the police that said drugs have taken off over the last month. Ice coming into the west."

Timmins nodded. "There has been an uptick in arrests here, and if I look I can get figures for the other districts."

"Do that."

"Do you think they're flying them in like last time?" he asked me. "Maybe on trucks?"

"No."

"What about manufacturing them here?"

My head bobbed slowly. "That could be a possibility. But to do that they would have to ship the ingredients in somehow. Have you heard anything?"

"Not really."

I reached for my cell. I dialed the number I had for Bomber and waited for it to ring.

"Yeah, what?"

"Have you found anything yet?"

"Nope."

"I have a theory for you. What if they were manufacturing them in the district?"

Bomber grunted. "There's a lot of land out there, Hayes. Could be possible though. Have to be on a station somewhere."

"They would need to ship a lot of gear in for manufacture," I pointed out. "You know anyone who might know something?"

"Maybe."

"Can you ask them?"

"I suppose."

"Thanks."

"Timmins, I have a job for you."

"Oh, yes?" He sounded a little offput.

"If they are manufacturing it in the district, they'll need somewhere to do it. Not here in town but maybe a station. Can you get a list of those in financial trouble?"

"Have you looked at the ground lately? That would be all of them."

I nodded. "Just the main ones. We can go through them later."

"What are you going to do?" he asked.

"I'm going to look at recent sales in the area. Maybe whoever is financing this bought a property as well."

There were four properties in the area that had sold within the past four months. I figured that would be more than enough time for whoever to set up. They ranged between a few hundred acres, right up to 20,000. All were sold by the same estate agent in town. Rural Regency.

I stared at the list and crossed off two. What drug boss was going to manufacture drugs on a property and employ hands to run it. No one with any brains. They could leave it dry, but my thinking was that would draw attention.

That left two. One at 500 and the other at 200. I brought up the two properties. Both were off back roads.

I made a note of their addresses. Then I went to the real estate to ask a couple of questions.

There were two people in the office. The receptionist and the agent. Small town, small office.

When I arrived, both were in the back room. After I rang the bell for assistance they appeared; the woman, a slim, attractive lass with—dare I say it—no, you imagine it, a rather revealing top on, minus a few buttons, looked at me and gave me an embarrassed smile. "Can I help you?"

"I can come back if I'm interrupting?" I said, embarrassing her further.

"No," said the estate agent. "Tina was just dictating something for me."

I'm sure she was. Even in times of despair, sometimes a man with a fast wit is required. "Is she any good at it?"

"Pardon?"

"Dictation?"

"Ah—yes, quite."

The girl named Tina was now the color of her smudged lipstick. One last little needle. I looked at her. "Did you find it hard?"

For a moment I thought she might faint. The agent had a wedding band on his finger, and I thought to myself that I was staring at another possible case.

"What can we do for you?" the agent asked.

"My name is Mark Hayes. I'm a private investigator. I—"

"You're him," Tina said, interrupting.

Small town fame. "As I was saying—"

"Are you working on something else?" she asked excitedly. "Has there been a murder?"

"Let the man speak, Tina," the estate agent reprimanded her. "Sorry, Hayes. I'm Glen Alan. This is my agency."

I nodded. "Yes, I am working on something and I'm hoping you can help me with it. I take it that you're the only agency in town?"

"Yes. The other one shut. A case of not enough business for two and too much for one. I'm looking to hire another salesperson."

I nodded. "You recently sold two properties." I gave him the addresses. "Can I ask you about the people who bought them?"

He suddenly looked alarmed, like I'd actually walked in on his receptionist blowing him. "I—ah—I—no, sorry, I can't tell you anything, really."

"I haven't asked you yet. I just need a name and how they paid."

Alan shook his head vigorously. "No, sorry, I can't tell you."

"Are you sure?"

"Yes, sorry."

I didn't want to do it, but sometimes you just need a little incentive to persuade some people. "Are you really, sure? I mean, I'd be discreet and all. Especially about the things that happen out in the back room. Just think, small town, loose lips—I'm sure the lips weren't but you know what I mean, right?"

He paled. "Oh, God."

"Are you saying that you'd tell everyone that I was sucking his dick when I wasn't doing no such thing?" Tina blurted out.

I stared at her. "Let's see. Open buttons on your blouse, smudged red lipstick, and I'm sure if Glen dropped his pants, he'd have a matching red ring around his Johnson, so, yes, I guess that is what I'm saying."

"Asshole," she hissed at me.

"I'm trying to do the town a favor," I replied.

"Go and die somewhere, that would be favor enough."

I nodded. "I just might do that yet."

"Enough, Tina," Alan snapped. "Get me the files on those properties."

"Fine," she huffed.

She returned after a couple of minutes and forced the folders into my hands. I went through them and found the two pieces of paper I wanted. "Could you copy these for me? Please?"

She grunted, snatching them from me. I heard her mutter, "You want me to suck your dick, too?"

Again, another couple of minutes and I said, "Thanks."

Then I left them to their cavorting.

Climbing into the Land Cruiser, I put my seatbelt on before sitting quietly to examine the papers I'd just acquired. One had a name on it, but the second one interested me more. It was a company. Sinock Farms. In my experience, those who wanted to hide something did it behind shell companies. They didn't use their names. I looked at the price paid and then after it was written the word, CASH.

I called Timmins. "I think I've found what I'm looking for."

"That was fast. How did you do it?"

"Caught the estate agent with his pants down."

"Glen was diddling Tina again, wasn't he?"

"In a fashion."

"What's your plan of attack now?"

"I'll call Bomber and have him look around. Meanwhile, I will look into the company that owns it."

"What's the name?" Timmins asked me curiously.

"Sinock Farms."

"Never heard of them."

"Any news on the drugs?"

"Not yet, I'm waiting on a call."

"I'll talk to you later."

Next, I called Bomber. "That was quick, I was just about to call you."

"You found something?"

"Sure did." Bomber sounded pleased with himself.

"So did I. You first."

"I talked to a friend, and he told me there were some funny shipments coming in."

"What kind of shipments?" I asked.

"Hydrochloric Acid, Lithium, Acetone, Toluene," Bomber said. "But here is the kicker, amongst all this stuff was Pseudoephedrine."

"How does your friend know all this stuff, Bomber?"

"Don't ask. I'm going to check it out."

"Did he give you a name?"

"No name," Bomber replied, "but there was a company on the manifest."

Thanks Bomber, your friend is a freight hauler. "What's the company?"

"Sinock Farms."

"Quite a coincidence," I shot back at him.

"You come up with that name, too?"

"Yes." I told him about the farm. "Wait for me, we'll go and check it out together."

"Fine." He told me where he was.

"I'll be there in five minutes."

"I'm not going anywhere."

CHAPTER FIFTEEN

I found Bomber where he told me he would be. From there we drove out of town, got off the main road, and followed a gravel one southwest for around ten kilometers. The land around us was relatively flat except for the occasional dry creek bed.

"Tell me about the chemicals," I said.

Bomber looked at me. "What do you want to know?"

"Where they came from?"

"Place in Dubbo. They were picked up from there."

"Who by?" I asked.

"I can't tell you that," Bomber replied. "What I can tell you is that the operation is professional."

"How professional?"

"They shipped the pseudoephedrine from overseas inside forty-fours. Which means they have someone inside customs. Before the stuff was picked up, the driver was stripped down and searched. Just in case."

"They wouldn't just do that to any courier, Bomber. The guy they had do it was obviously dodgy."

"Yeah, well."

"And he brought the stuff out here?"

"Yes."

"What did he see?" I asked.

"Not a lot. It was dark when he arrived. Four or five guys, big, ugly bastards, he said. But get this, they were dressed as bikers."

I frowned. "Dressed as bikers, or were bikers?"

"His exact words were, ain't like no bloody bikers I ever saw before."

I thought for a moment. They were either not bikers or they were, and Bomber was trying to throw me off and was leading me into a trap. In which case there was a good chance I would wind up dead.

"Bomber, when we were in Sydney, did you hear of any trouble between the Taipans and Franchi?"

"No more than usual."

I nodded.

But as we got closer to our destination a few low ridges rose out of the plain as well as the odd thicket of trees.

I slowed as we came to the gateway. Leading away from it was a narrow, graded track meandering around a small hill dotted with trees.

"Keep going," Bomber snapped. "Don't stop."

"What's wrong?" I asked him, easing my foot back down on the gas pedal.

"There's someone on that hill. In the trees. I saw the flash off something. Maybe binoculars."

We kept going along the road with Bomber scanning the trees on the hill. "I think I can make him out."

"Bugger. We need to find another way in."

"Leave it. I'll come back later on my bike. I'll see if I can find out what is going on."

"Be dangerous coming back out here on your own," I pointed out to him.

"Nothing I never done before."

I nodded. "All right. Let's go back to town."

I let Bomber out with a word of warning. "Be careful and watch your back."

He grunted and closed the door. My stomach growled and I realized that I hadn't had lunch so made a beeline for Elvira's place. No sense in going hungry. I walked inside and the first person I saw was Tommy Hansen. He glanced up at me before dropping his gaze.

"Are you causing trouble again?" I asked him.

"Nuh."

"What are you up to?"

"Nothing."

Elvira came in from out the back. "Hi, Mark."

"Elvira, the kid causing trouble?"

"No, no. He's waiting on some food. I gather that's why you are here."

"Yes, please. The usual."

"Pie and chips coming up."

In the time that it took her to get my food ready, Tommy Hansen collected his and disappeared. Elvira passed my order to me, and I gave her the money she asked for. As she put it into the cash drawer, she hesitated, looking at a bill I gave her. She shook her head. "This one has got red dye on it. Looks like dye, I wonder how it got there."

Red dye? "Can I have a look at that for a moment, Elvira?"

She passed it back to me. I stared at it for a long moment. Then it came to me. I don't know why I hadn't thought of it before. I dug out another bill from my pocket and replaced it with the one I had in my hand.

"There you go, Elvira. I'll keep the other one, it might be lucky."

Outside, the heat was easing, clouds were building. Which was a comfort, for the days of late had been shit. I hated heat yet I chose to live in a bloody furnace. I sat at the small table that Nicole and I had shared the last time we were there together. As I ate, I stared at the $20 bill. What I wanted to do was charge off and ask questions, but I really needed to eat.

I had just finished when a Commodore pulled up at an angle to the carpark. Not a problem, the driver couldn't park right. What surprised me was that Higgins climbed out of the passenger seat in his neat suit. He stared at me and said, "We need to talk."

The money would have to wait.

The pub dining lounge was quiet. The lunch crowd had gone and now it was empty. I sat with Higgins in a corner away from prying eyes.

"Tell me what you know," he said to me.

I nodded. "Someone is cooking drugs in the district. Meth."

He just stared at me. "Keep going."

"I think they might be the same people that killed Franchi's two men and took a shot at me. I also think they were the ones who put the money in Nicole's account. The thing is, they're posing as bikers, and I don't know why. Bryce told me that drugs were popping up all across the western districts."

Higgins's head bobbed up and down. "That's right. We think that they're cooking somewhere around here."

"I think I might have found it."

The copper sat forward in his seat. "Where?"

"A farm outside of town. Bomber Hansen is checking it out."

"Bomber Hansen?"

"That's right."

He wasn't happy. "Why the hell would you do something like that?"

"Because he's useful. The farm was delivered a load of chemicals recently and also pseudoephedrine as well. I only know that because of him. He's not part of it."

"He's a damned biker, of course he's part of it. If not that then some other illegal shit."

I stared at him. "I've told you what I know, how about you tell me what this is really about. You've gone out of your way to have me dig about to see what I can find. You should have your task force out here, but what I think is that you're afraid of spooking someone."

"You're a smart man, Hayes. You actually might be right."

"Who is it?"

"Let's just say it's someone important and if I bring my taskforce in here then it might spook him. That's if he's even here."

"Christ, Higgins, what the hell have you got me into? You said we needed to talk, yet you've given me nothing." I paused. Then something else dawned on me. I'm smart like that. If enough shit goes into my head, I eventually decode it. "Are you using me as bait, Higgins?"

"Whatever do you mean?"

Sarcasm. It wasn't much, but it was there. "What I mean is that you put me on this because you know I won't let it go because of what happened to Nicole. You're hoping that I will draw whoever it is out into the open where you lot can swoop in and pick whoever it is up. How am I doing?"

"You left one thing out," Higgins replied.

"What was that?"

"The fact that you were targeted before we picked you up."

Now I was angry. "You knew I was going to be targeted?" I snarled maybe a little too loudly.

"There were whispers but nothing concrete. By the time we had it, the job was already done."

"But you're still not telling me who it is," I pointed out.

"No, we want your concentration on the job at hand. Not have you running off on a tangent and screwing it up."

"Then fuck you, I'm not doing anymore."

"Then we'll put you in jail for receiving payment for illegal activities," Higgins said calmly.

"What?"

"You received forty grand from Salvador Franchi as payment for illegal activities. That alone should keep you tied up for a while even if it can't be proved."

"You bastard," I grated. "How the hell—"

"We are monitoring Franchi, remember?"

I shook my head in resignation. "What do you want me to do?"

"I want you to keep *doing* what you are doing. Confirm where the meth is being made and report back."

"I'm just a PI, Higgins."

"And that is what we want. Investigate, Hayes. Use all of that talent you have."

I stared at him. "Now I'm talented?"

Higgins got to his feet. "Just do it."

"I don't have much choice, do I?"

I walked into the roadhouse and joined the lineup. It crawled slowly to the counter where a tired-eyed man looked up at me and said, "What pump?"

"No pump, I'm looking for Cheryl," I replied.

"She's not on today."

"Do you know where I might find her?"

He stared at me as though he was denying me the answer. I looked at the name tag. "Please, Ted, I need to ask her some questions."

"What about?"

"Hey, are you going to pay, mate, or what?" a young man asked from behind me.

I took out my ID. "I'm Mark Hayes. I'm investigating what happened to Sergeant Nicole Berger."

It was a slight lie for the time but, anyhow. He looked at me. "It don't look like a badge."

"It's not, I'm a PI."

"What did you say your name was?"

"Are you going to bloody hurry up?" the young man snapped.

I turned and gave him my best displeased stare. "Respect, huh?"

"Screw you."

My fist moved a short distance but with a good lot of power. In spite of my diet, I still had a little strength. It found the soft flesh of his middle and he doubled over. He gagged and gasped for air. Patting him on the back I said, "Breathe through it, son."

I turned back to Ted. "I'm Mark Hayes."

"I heard of you." The comment was becoming commonplace. "Cheryl will probably be out at the lake with her friends. They get out there occasionally on her days off. I thought I heard her say something about it."

"Thank you, Ted."

"Good luck. I hope you find who did it."

I turned and patted my new friend on the shoulder as he started to regain his breath. I gave him a smile and said, "Respect."

My drive out to the lake took around half an hour. I turned off the asphalt and hit the gravel without a crunch as the 4X4 took the drop easily with its height, unlike what would happen with the Monaro every time.

I followed the road which became a track to the lake and stopped. Friar's Lake was full, unlike when the missing girls were discovered. It happened in a cycle. The storms would come, and the lake would fill. Then as the year wore on until the next storm season, it would slowly dry up. That was how the killers disposed of the bodies. There were sinks in the bottom of the lake, kind of like mushy quicksand which never dried out. They would dump the bodies of their victims in there and forget about them.

I came to a stop where they had parked their cars. There were maybe ten or so young people sitting around together drinking beer and generally having a good time. Some had wet hair and had been enjoying what the lake had to offer before it dried again.

I closed the door of the 4X4 and approached them. They were a mixed bunch. Young men and women, Caucasian and Aboriginal. Out here the young people didn't worry about the color of another's skin. They took each other as they came. Not like some of the old breed.

"What do you want?" a young bloke asked me, a sharp edge to his voice.

I was classed as the old breed.

"I'm here looking for Cheryl," I replied.

"What for?"

"Mind your own business, Eric," Cheryl said as she climbed to her feet. She had a can of Carlton Draught in her hand. "Take no notice of him. You wanting to know more about them bikers?"

I shook my head and dug out the bank note with the red on it. I held it out and asked, "Do you remember where you got this from?"

She took the money and examined it, her mind ticking back to the day she got it.

"Hey," one of the others called out. "You want to give money away, you could hand it to me."

I glanced at the smart-assed young man. "You're not my type. If you were, I'd be having all your money."

The connotation brought forth a howl of delight from the others. I gave the young man a wink and he turned red. Anger? Embarrassment? I wasn't sure but it made him shut up.

"Now I remember," Cheryl said to me. Her face lit up with pleasure. "It was Gerald Long."

"Are you sure?"

"Yes. I remember him saying that he had a red pen leak in his pocket when he handed it over."

I nodded. "You don't happen to know where he lives, do you?"

"Old Dog Flats."

"Where is that?"

"Out west about twenty minutes. There is a sign that points you in the right direction. It's a gravel road."

I smiled at her. "You're a gem, Cheryl. I'll dance at your wedding."

"Liar. How is the sarge?"

I gave a solemn look. "No change yet," I told her. "But Nic is tough, she'll pull through."

"I'm sure she will. Would you like a beer?"

Shaking my head, I said, "No thanks. You lot don't

want an old codger like me cramping your style. I'll go home and cook myself some dinner."

"Oh?"

"Yeah, steak and chips from the pub," I said with a laugh as I walked away.

CHAPTER SIXTEEN

I had dinner with everyone's favorite newspaper reporter. In fact, he phoned me as I was walking into the pub, and he somehow wormed his way into a dinner invitation. Not that it mattered because we needed to talk anyway.

I was starting on my second beer when he arrived. I was in the lounge and already the smell of frying food had filtered its way through the place, making me even hungrier. When Timmins sat down, we ordered. Instead of steak I went with a mixed grill. Sausages, eggs, bacon, lamb chops, chips; all the good stuff. The intrepid reporter ordered some kind of rabbit food salad with chicken.

Looking at him, I asked, "What did you find out?"

"Sinock Farms is owned by an overseas corporation."

"Of course, it is."

"I looked into it as far as I could and couldn't find any names," Timmins informed me.

"Where are they based?"

"Brunei."

The food I was about to put in my mouth stopped halfway. "Are you sure?"

He nodded. "Yes, why?"

I thought in silence before saying, "Just curious. What else?"

"Not much. I asked around but came up with nothing else. What about you?"

As I finished my meal, I told him about Bomber and the farm. He seemed surprised that I let him go on his own. "Are you sure he'll be all right?"

"I hope so," I replied. I put my hand in my pocket and took out the bank note. "Tell me, what do you make of this?"

Timmins took the money and looked it over. He paused for a moment, his hooded eyes staring at the dye mark. "Is that what I think it is?"

I nodded. "It could be."

"Dye?"

"Yes."

"The armored truck robbery?"

With a shrug of tired shoulders, I said, "I don't know."

"Are you going to report it?"

I hadn't thought it all the way through. "I'm not sure. I might look into it a bit further just in case."

"Be careful."

"Do you know a Gerald Long?" I asked.

"Sure," Timmins replied.

I waited patiently for him to continue but he just stared at me. "Well?" I asked.

"Oh, sorry. He lives out at Old Dog Flats on his family property. His father died last year from a heart attack. Stress from the hard life of running a failing place. With him gone, Gerald had to step up. His mother left a short time after, couldn't take it."

"He's out there on his own?"

Timmins nodded. "Apart from a few hands. They're still bleeding money, but Gerald won't leave it go."

My head bobbed once again. I took a pull of my beer and asked, "Who does he hang out with?"

"No one anymore. Used to be with Bluey Timms, Nellie Brown, Jimmy Morrison, Jim Kelly, and Tom and Betty Mason. They were all tight."

"Not anymore?"

"Not after his father died and he broke up with Betty."

"Wait, he used to go out with Betty Mason?"

"Sure. But they broke up just before his father died," Timmins explained. "Kind of killed the vibe."

"Do you know why?" I asked.

"No idea. Whisper was another bloke, but I never saw her with one."

I had a fair idea who it was. "What about the others?"

"Not much to tell. They still have a beer together every now and then. Nellie is an on again, off again proposition for Jimmy Morrison."

"How does Tom Mason fit into the group?" I inquired.

"How do you mean?" Timmins asked.

"Every group has an Alpha male, right? Just curious."

The newspaper journo nodded his understanding. "I guess you would say that Tom was the Alpha male. Why all the questions?"

I told him about the bull.

"You think Tom was responsible for it?"

"With help."

"Shit."

"Tell me this: how many were responsible for the armored truck heist?" I asked him.

Timmins frowned. "Five, I think. Professional crew by the sounds of it."

I stared at him. "Any of them had any military experience?"

"Only one," Timmins replied.

"Who?"

"Tom Mason."

Wow. The evening was full of surprises. "I thought he was land locked on the station?"

"No, he got out for a few years, did some army stuff. Did a peacekeeping tour in Africa. At one point his company was ambushed by some terrorist organization I can't even pronounce."

"Why did he get out?"

"Had enough, I guess."

I drank the last of my beer. "Is Jack Mason Tom's father?"

Timmins paused. I could see the inner turmoil inside him through his eyes. The secret was burned deep within the town. "No."

I asked no more. I had the answer I wanted. Now all I wanted to do was go home, ring Linda, and find out how —the cell in my pocket buzzed. I took it out and looked at the screen. Speak of the devil as they say. I hit the answer button and said, "Hey, Linda."

"Hey, handsome."

The voice was dry, raspy, but it was her. It was Nicole.

It was so wonderful to hear her voice. I felt tears well in my eyes as my emotions which had been sunk deep inside came to the surface. "Hey, yourself."

"How are you doing?" she asked me.

"Bugger me. How are you?" I shot back at her.

"Tired."

"Don't go back to sleep," I blurted out. "I'll drive over to Dubbo and catch a plane tonight."

I heard her dry chuckle. "No. Linda tells me you're very busy."

"Stuff work." There was a long silence. "How is the baby?"

"I was hoping you would ask," she said. "I was scared you wouldn't."

"Not ask about the two most important people in my life? I don't think so."

"The baby is fine. Tough like its father."

"Its mother you mean. What did the doctors say?"

More silence before Nic said, "Sorry, baby, I'm just tired. Love you."

"Love you, too."

There was a rustle and then Linda's voice came over the line. "Hello, Mark."

"Is she alright?"

"Yes, just tired. Don't worry."

"When did she wake up?"

"Earlier this afternoon. I didn't want to tell you until we knew what was happening," she explained.

"And?"

"And, according to the doctor she will be fine. Both her and the baby."

"I need to get back to Sydney," I said to her.

"Just wait for a while, Mark. There is nothing you can do. I'll take care of her. Once she is stronger then come. Right now, I guess Nicole needs you doing what you're doing. Nothing worse than a doting male getting in the way."

"Are you sure?" I asked.

"Of course. You know, the more I talk to you, the more I think I like you."

"Sorry, I'm taken."

She chuckled. "Sorry, I'm a lesbian."

"OK, you win."

"I'll call you tomorrow, Mark. Take care."

"You, too, Linda. Give her a kiss for me."

"I promise."

The call disconnected and I looked across at Timmins. He smiled. "Good news?"

"Yes, and if I see it in tomorrow's paper I'll know where it came from."

"I'm sure that the people of Friar's Lake would like to know that she is fine."

I shook my head. "Not yet, George."

He nodded. "All right, I'll let it go. But right now, I'm going home."

"Me, too," I said, agreeing with his idea. However, I knew I wouldn't sleep too well. I was too amped after talking to Nic.

The bullet came out of the night like an angry hornet you used to see on the old cartoon shows. It fanned my face and slammed into the front wall of the pub. Almost immediately I grabbed Timmins and dragged him down behind a parked vehicle. A Ford Falcon with a bug mesh over its grill.

"Stay down," I snapped at him as a second bullet slammed into the rear window of the Ford, shattering it then blowing out through the front one. "High-powered rifle."

"What?" Timmins blurted out. "Is someone shooting at us?"

"You could say that."

"Shit a brick. Why would someone shoot at us?"

In the yellow haze from the pub's veranda light being

circled by a thousand bugs of the night, I stared at the newspaper man. "Why indeed?"

It took another few heartbeats before the penny dropped. "Oh, right."

Another shot. One shooter, not like before when Nicole's home was sprayed. In the distance I could hear police sirens. It hadn't taken long for word to get around. The shooting stopped, then came the sound of a bike. Not a chopper, a dirt bike receding into the distance. Then the police arrived.

So much for an early night. Such and Waters questioned me until two in the morning. I'm sure there was no need, but I could tell they were more than a little pissed off with me. Possibly the fact that to them I was seemingly untouchable didn't help.

"Did you see who it was?"

"No."

"Any idea who it might have been?"

"No."

"Did you see anything at all?"

"No."

"Hear anything?"

"Motorbike."

Such stared at me. Back in the day I might have asked her out for the simple fact she intrigued me. Even though she was Australian, I could see that she had Asian roots somewhere in her past. "A motorbike?"

"Yes."

"Pissed anyone off lately?"

"Dumb frigging question," I growled.

"Well, shit, Mark, you're not giving us much to go on,

are you?" Such growled back at me. "Any idea what sort of bike?"

"Trail."

"Not road?"

"No."

Once more her stare focused on me. "Why are you so special?" Her words were terse.

"I'm not special."

"Someone sure as shit thinks you are."

"Not me."

"What has Stewart Higgins got you doing?" Waters asked.

"Who?"

His face screwed up with frustration. "Don't bullshit me, Hayes. Higgins has you doing something."

"Even if he has, you know I'm not going to tell you."

Such rose to her feet from the other side of the table. "So he has got you doing something. Even for him this is highly irregular. Maybe even illegal."

I shrugged. "Maybe I'm an informant."

They left it at that and questioned me until they'd had enough. Jace showed me out and once we were outside in the cold darkness, I said to him, "Nicole's awake."

He was surprised by the news. "Really? Is she all right?"

"As far as I know."

"That's great, Mark."

"Yeah, it is." I paused. "Robbery and Serious Crimes Task Force in town?"

"Yes."

"Any progress?"

"No. Not that I know of. They don't tell me much."

"Same shit, huh?" I asked.

"Yes." It was his turn to pause. "Mark, what are you mixed up in?"

"Such put you up to that?"

He looked guilty. "Sorry."

"All I'm doing is trying to find out who shot Nic."

He nodded. "Yeah, don't blame you. Take care, Mark. Watch your back."

"Thanks, Jace. Oh, and keep the news about Nicole under your hat for the time being. The last thing she needs is coppers crawling all over her for something she didn't do."

Jace knew he was talking about the money. And even though he was duty-bound to divulge the information, he said, "They won't learn it from me."

I went home and climbed into bed. The last time I looked at the clock on the small dresser it said three. The bashing on the front door came at one minute past.

My hand went under the pillow for the Glock. It slid out and I climbed from the wide bed. The timber frame creaked as I left the mattress and then hurriedly pulled on my pants. I padded towards the front door and another crashing pounding on the door.

"Who is it?" I asked cautiously, the handgun raised.

"It's me, open the frigging door."

Bomber, and he sounded different.

I found out why when I opened the door and he almost fell in. He'd been shot and was losing blood. "What the hell happened?"

"I got bloody careless," he grunted. "Help me inside."

His shirt was soaked with blood and in the light his face looked ashen. "You need to get to a hospital."

"Bugger that. I'll be a'right, my old lady has made me bleed worse than this."

I highly doubted it. I put him on the lounge and knew instantly I would be docking his pay to buy a new one. Stuff him, if he wanted to bleed all over it, he could pay. I got his shirt off him and saw the large gaping gash that a bullet had ripped in the flesh of his side. "That will need cleaning."

"Then do it."

"Yeah, wait here."

I went into the kitchen and looked through the cupboards. I took out a bottle of white vinegar and poured it into a bowl. Then I filled it with hot water, got an old hand towel for a rag, and went back into the lounge room. "This is going to hurt you more than me," I said to Bomber.

"Just get it done."

Ten minutes later, I said, "It's going to need stitching."

"Whatever."

You can never find a needle and thread when you need one. So, I improvised. It's amazing what you can find around a home to close a wound. Once I had what I needed I went back into the living room and said, "I'm going to have to improvise."

Bomber took one look at the Phillips steam iron I was holding and shook his head. "Fuck me, what are you going to do with that?"

"Whatever I have to."

"Shit."

I plugged it in, and it heated rather quickly. Once it was hot, I took it, still plugged in and turned on, and hovered over Bomber. "You might want to brace yourself."

"Got any whiskey?"

I shoved a cushion at him. "Bite on this."

He stuffed a corner in his mouth and bit down.

"You ready."

"Just hurry the f—argh!"

He passed out.

It was daylight when he woke up. I had achieved some sleep in one of the armchairs while he was out of it.

His first words were, "You could have warned me it was going to hurt."

"Thought that was self-explanatory. Hot iron, soft flesh, not suited to enjoyment."

"Yeah. What time is it?"

"Six-thirty."

"Got a coffee?"

"I'll put the jug on. Then you can tell me what happened."

I made the coffees and took them back into the living room. Bomber was still awake, and the color had returned to his face. I gave him the cup and he grasped it with two hands, a slight tremor in them both. He took a sip and pulled a face. "Stick with being a PI."

"Screw you. Tell me what happened."

"I managed to get close to the farmhouse in the dark and decided to have a look around. The blokes working out there were dressed like bikers but they sure as shit aren't. I managed to get a look at their operation before they rumbled me. Well set up, cost a lot of money."

"Don't bikers have a lot of money?" I asked him.

"This setup was different. There's money, and then there's *money*. They were carrying automatic weapons. The guy in charge wore a suit and was always on a phone talking to someone."

"Do you know who?"

"No."

"Automatic weapons you say?"

"Yes."

Possibly the people who shot up Nicole's. I thought for a moment longer. The ones who shot up Nicole's had automatic weapons. The ambushers on the road had rifles, and the incident outside the pub was a rifle as well.

"Bloody hell," I muttered.

"What?" Bomber asked.

"I've got two lots of people trying to kill me."

The wounded biker chuckled. "Man, aren't you the lucky one?"

I nodded, my face grim. "Yes, real bloody lucky."

"Where are you going?" Bomber asked me, staring at the Weatherby rifle I was holding in my hand.

"To have a look out at that farm," I replied.

"Are you crazy or something?" Bomber struggled to sit up. "I'm coming with you."

"No. You stay right there."

There was a knock on the door. I answered it and let Timmins in. He glanced at the rifle. "You going to war?"

"Not yet."

We went into the living room. "Bomber, Timmins here is going to keep an eye on you."

"I don't need no frigging babysitter," he growled. His harsh stare focused on the newspaperman.

"Maybe he's right," Timmins replied meekly.

"Don't let him get to you. He bleeds just like the rest of us."

"Maybe you should leave it up to the police."

"I'll be fine. Once I confirm that they're still there I'll call the police then."

"You figure they might be gone?" Timmins asked.

I looked at Bomber. "It's a good possibility."

"What are you blaming me for?" the biker growled.

"Just behave yourself."

"Yes, mother."

CHAPTER SEVENTEEN

I observed the farm from the top of the low ridge I had managed to circle around to on foot. From the looks of it, I could have driven right up to the farmhouse. How I was going to tell Higgins the fantastic news, you will notice the sarcasm, was a painful thought. Stuff it, Bryce could tell him.

I stood up, sky lining myself against the cloudless sky. I put the Weatherby back up to my shoulder and swept the large station yard one last time.

Nothing.

I started trudging down the forward slope, making my way around rocks and past trees. Dust kicked up from my boots with each step. Even though we'd had a little rain, the furnace overhead dried it out in no time.

Above me in a tree, a crow made its throaty sound like the alien from the movie *Predator* before it opened its beak wide to release its annoying caw. It was answered by a Sulphur-Crested Cockatoo in another tree to my right.

When I reached the flat ground, I kept walking, not fast, just cautiously. Halfway there a dry creek bed cut across in front of me. The banks were rounded from erosion and were easily navigated. I crossed it and kept on going.

Upon reaching the yard, I stopped. I slung the rifle over my shoulder and drew the Glock. Everything was silent apart from the birds in the distance. It gave the whole scene an eerie feel like in the movies. All that was missing was the tense music and the small gust of wind which whipped up a cloud of dust. However, we still had flies by the thousand.

I checked the house first. Whoever had been in there had definitely left in a hurry. I went room by room but found nothing which told me who they were.

Back outside I surveyed the two large sheds opposite. While I'd been inside, a slight breeze had sprung up, hot, almost suffocating. Glancing at my watch I noted the time. It was almost ten-thirty. It was going to be a damn hot day again.

The first shed I went into was vacant. Nothing in it at all. It was all concrete floor and nothing else apart from the truck marks where one had been backed in, leaving behind the grit it had picked up on the way in. When I went back outside, I looked down into the dust and dirt and found the same tire marks and boot prints everywhere. Just another sign they left in a hurry.

The second shed was different. It had been used to store chemicals and there were still empty drums inside. Empty drums and a body.

It was the corpse of a man, early thirties, scruffy face, well built, wearing jeans and a flannelette shirt with the sleeves torn out. No tattoos, no piercings, no other marks which would confirm him as a biker. Because he wasn't a biker.

He'd been shot twice in the chest, once in the head.

Making sure. Obviously, he had paid for Bomber's intrusion and escape.

The question now was, where did they go?

I reached into my pocket for my cell. Jackpot. I had signal. Around Friar's Lake it was a game of is there or isn't there. I dialed in the number for Bryce.

"What's up?"

"I have a situation."

I went on to tell him about it.

"And now they've flown the coop," the detective muttered.

"It would seem so."

"Higgins is going to fucking love this."

The call disconnected. I guessed that was it. The criminals were spooked and now gone. My time was over.

Or so I thought.

My cell buzzed and I looked at the screen. Immediately I thought of Higgins and the anger about to come down the line at me like a runaway freight train. I pulled the Land Cruiser over and answered.

"Mark Hayes."

"Mark, it's Grandma Mary."

Surprise.

"Hi, is everything OK?"

"Not really." There was more than a hint of worry to her voice. "I need to see you."

"I'm sorry, Mary, but I'm in the middle of something at the minute." I hated saying no.

"It's important, Mark," she insisted. "You really need to come out here."

I sighed. After the night I'd had, and now the shit

with the farm, the last thing I wanted to do was drive out to Hampton. "Mary—"

"It's Helen."

Shit! "On my way."

Upon arrival, Hampton lived up to its bustling best. A blue heeler dog walking along main street. Right in the middle, making me swerve around it. Luckily there was a break in traffic at the time and I was able to perform the maneuver safely.

I negotiated my way to Grandma Mary's and pulled into the drive. When I got out, I made sure I had the Glock tucked securely inside my pants.

The door opened before I could knock. Grandma Mary filled the frame and then stepped aside as I reached the top of the steps. "She's in the kitchen."

I made my way through the house to the kitchen where Helen Miller waited for me. When I saw her, I wasn't sure I was seeing right. Her hair was shorter and a different color. But when I saw the face, the freckles, I knew. The fourteen-year-old exploded off the chair and came into my arms. I wrapped them around her tightly and said, "You've grown."

"You're still alive," she replied.

I eased her back and looked into her eyes. There were tears there and a look of relief on her face. "Why wouldn't I be?"

"He told me you were dead."

"Agosti?" I asked, meaning Pete Agosti, the crime boss formerly of Australia but having been on the run in another country for some months now.

"Yes. Him and mum."

"Well, I'm not."

Her arms wrapped around me again and remained that way for a few minutes before she let me go. I looked once more into her eyes and asked, "Where is he, Helen?"

"I'm not sure."

"Is he here making drugs?"

"Yes, I think so."

"Your mother?"

She went silent.

I could see the trouble in her eyes. "Helen, where's your mother?"

"She—I think she's dead."

"What happened?"

"I think he killed her," she said softly. "They were fighting and then she went out and never came home."

"Where?"

"Brunei."

"Are you sure?" I asked her. "It wouldn't be the first time she shot through on you."

"I don't know."

I nodded. "I need you to tell me what's going on."

"Mark," Grandma Mary cautioned me, "I don't think now is a good time."

"I'm sorry but I need to do this. Someone is manufacturing drugs in the area. I found them but now they're gone. I think they are the same ones who killed the two men in the car and are responsible for Nic getting shot." I looked at Helen again. "Please, Helen, start at the beginning."

"OK. After we left here, we went to Brunei. Pete was running things from there."

"His operation?" I asked.

"Yes. He kept it to himself, but I'd overhear him and mum talking. Anyway, one day a man showed up. I found out later he was Australian. A policeman."

I frowned. "What was an Australian policeman doing in Brunei?"

"He had a proposition for Pete. Something to do with setting up a factory out west. Out here. I never heard it all."

"Sounds like you heard enough."

"Pete wanted him to get rid of you, too," Helen said. "Paid him to do it. But he failed."

"Nicole," I muttered.

"Yes. I guess so."

"Did you hear what the copper's name was?" I asked her.

She nodded. "Bryce."

This just kept getting better. "How did you get here?"

"I ran off. Last night with all the trouble at the farm I just ran. Hitched a ride this morning and came here."

"Agosti was at the farm?"

"Yes."

"Why did he keep you around?" I asked her.

"I don't know."

She was lying, I could see it in her face. "Helen?"

She hesitated.

"Why did he keep you around?" I asked again.

"Because Pete Agosti is my real father."

Well shit. "He's going to want to find you."

Helen nodded. "I know. That's why I asked Grandma Mary to call you."

"All right, we need to get you out of here. I'll make a call."

"No. I'm coming with you."

"That's fine but I have to call the man I'm working for."

I went out the back door into the yard. It had obviously suffered the worst of it through lack of rain because there were large patches of dirt with scattered clumps of dead grass on them. I took out the cell and dialed. As soon as I heard the click, I said, "You bastard."

"I should be saying that to you," Higgins replied.

"If you were in front of me, I'd punch you in the frigging mouth."

"I gather you've figured it out."

"Pete Agosti? You couldn't tell me it was him?" I snarled.

"How did you find out?" he asked me.

"His daughter."

"What daughter?" I could hear the confusion in his voice.

"Helen Miller. She escaped him and reached out to me."

"I'll be buggered. We need to talk to her."

"Stuff you. She stays with me. Last time I handed her over to cops we know what happened. And I hear there are more rats in the ranks."

"You can't keep her safe, Mark," Higgins said.

He was right. "Bullshit I can't."

"How?"

"I have a way," I said. "How about you tell me what the hell is going on."

"I'll be there before night. Expect me."

I went back inside. "I'll take you somewhere safe."

"Where?" Helen asked.

"Somewhere out of sight." I looked at Grandma Mary. "It's better all round this way."

She nodded. "Yes, I understand."

"Do you have any clothes?" I asked Helen."

"No."

"I'll have to figure something out. Let's go." I turned

back to the old woman. "Thank you, Mary."

"They're coming, Mark. I can feel it."

I nodded. If there was one thing I'd learned since knowing the old Aboriginal woman, it was to take note when she told you something. "I'll be ready."

When I got back to Friar's Lake, I found Bomber where I'd left him and Timmins sitting in the chair keeping an eye on him. It was the latter who reacted first when he saw Helen. "Oh, my God."

"Yes," I agreed before looking at Bomber. "I need your help again."

"After you hit me with a steam iron?"

"Stopped you bleeding, didn't it?"

He sighed. "What do you want?"

I pointed at Helen. "I need her kept safe."

"What did she do?" Hansen asked.

"Ran away from her father."

"Who is her father?" Bomber asked.

"Pete Agosti."

"*The* Pete Agosti?"

I nodded. "Yes. It was his people who shot you last night. I'm betting it was him on the phone."

"All right," Bomber said. "But you're not going to like what I suggest."

"At this point in time I'm all out of ideas," I told him.

"Get me the phone."

"Who are you ringing?"

"Mongrel."

I hesitated. He was calling the club president of the Taipans to help watch over a vulnerable girl. Bomber could see my inner turmoil. "She'll be safer with the Taipans than with anyone else, Mark."

"Where?" I asked.

"Dubbo or Sydney."

"Are you sure he will take it on?" I asked.

"I can only ask," he replied. "Might cost a bob or two."

Grabbing the phone, I handed it over. Bomber made the call which took all of two minutes. When he disconnected, he said, "He'll organize it. She'll be picked up after dark. Taken to Dubbo. Mongrel will fly out himself and escort her to Sydney."

"No," Helen blurted out. "I'm staying here."

I turned and looked at her. "I can't protect you like these guys can, Helen. No one will mess with them. Not even your father. Once this is over, I'll come and get you myself. I promise."

"I don't want to."

"It's either that or go back to your father. I can't protect you from him at the moment. This is your best bet."

She looked worried but relented, her face sagging. "OK."

Higgins arrived before dark as he said he would. He came inside and left his driver in the vehicle. I looked at him and shook my head. "You can't leave the kids in the car, Higgins."

"Fine, tell him to come in."

I looked over at Timmins who'd been to his work and then returned. "Would you?"

"Why not."

The copper stared at Bomber Hansen who was still on the sofa. "What's he doing here?"

"He got shot. Didn't Bryce tell you?"

"He might have mentioned it in passing. I was hoping he'd be dead. I see that was too much to wish for."

"Screw you, copper," Bomber shot back at him.

Next, he focused on Helen. "It is good to see you safe. Are you alright?"

She nodded. "Yes."

"What are you going to do with her?" he asked me.

"Some people are coming to pick her up, soon."

"What people?" Higgins asked.

"Ones that will keep her safe. That's all you need to know. Now, tell me what the bloody hell is going on."

Higgins sighed. "As you know, Pete Agosti is back in the country."

"No shit."

"You also know why he came home. We just didn't know where he had his setup. We knew it was around here somewhere, but we couldn't go stomping around like bloody elephants and risk spooking him." He looked at Bomber. "Not that it matters now. Anyway, the other part to the equation was that we knew we had a crooked copper inside the department, but we didn't know who. We're still not sure."

"It's Bryce," I supplied. "He went to Brunei and met with Agosti."

Higgins nodded. "He was in the frame with a couple of others. Shit."

"You had no idea?" I asked.

"No. Anyway, to begin with, pieces of intelligence filtered their way through to our taskforce about someone in Brunei shipping ingredients into the country. We didn't know who or where to. I reached out to the Feds, and they managed to come up with a picture of the man they thought was responsible."

Higgins reached into his pocket and took out the photograph. He passed it to me. I didn't recognize the man at all but the person standing beside him I would have known anywhere. It was Helen. I glanced at him.

"Yes, we had trouble recognizing him, too. But it was the girl who gave us a clue."

I passed it to Helen. She looked at it and said, "We were shopping. Mum was inside the store."

"The feds were keeping an eye on him, but he suddenly just disappeared along with Helen."

"Do you know what happened to my mother?" Helen asked.

Higgins shook his head. "I'm sorry, Helen. We're not sure, but we believe that Agosti killed her."

She burst into tears, and I put my arm around her, pulling her close. I looked at Higgins. "Are you sure?"

He nodded. "Afraid so."

"What about the hit on me?"

"When that surfaced, we knew he was in the country. I mean, after he disappeared we figured he was coming this way, but when the hit happened we knew he was here. I guess he still holds a grudge."

"What about Franchi's men?" I asked.

"Collateral damage, I think. It's possible that they were seen by whoever was watching you. Maybe Agosti got the wrong idea and had them taken out of the equation."

"You could have told me."

"I agree, we fucked up. I'm sorry."

"Great. At least I know one lot responsible for trying to kill me."

Higgins frowned. "What do you mean?"

"The first crew that tried to kill me had automatic weapons. Agosti's men. The second had rifles. The third was a single shooter also with a rifle. I'm starting to think that people around here don't like me."

"I don't," said Bomber with a pained grin.

"So, you have three separate lots of shooters trying to kill you, is that what you are saying?"

"That's exactly what I'm saying."

Higgins's cell rang. He answered it and immediately his face turned grim. After a few terse sentences he hung up. "Well, you won't have to worry about Bryce anymore. He just turned up dead in the motel he was staying in. That was the Dubbo police. I need to go."

"What about Agosti?" I almost demanded.

"In the wind once more. Not much we can do until he surfaces."

"Shit."

"Things do have a habit of going that way when they get out of hand."

"He's not going to go anywhere, you know," I said to Higgins. "If he still thinks Helen is here, he'll keep looking. After all, she is his daughter."

"Then you'd better keep on your toes, because he still hasn't finished with you, either."

Not all bikers ride bikes all the time.

Never a truer word was spoken. Some drive dark vans. As was the case of the three bikers who visited Nicole's house a little after eight that evening.

They parked in the drive and climbed out. Two men of average height and the third who looked like he had the Hulk and King Kong for parents. His arms, like the others, were covered in tattoos. His goatee came down to his chest, and at a guess I would say he topped out at six-six, six-seven. His companions were about ten inches shorter than him but just as imposing. However, it was the big one who did all the talking.

"My name is Dennis," he told me. "My friends call me

something else, but we won't go into that. I was told to come here to help a little lady in trouble."

Helen took a step back. Dennis grinned warmly. "No need to be afraid, we're here to keep you safe."

"Who sent you?" I asked.

"What?" He looked confused.

"I need to be sure," I replied, my hand going to the Glock behind my back. "Who sent you."

Dennis nodded. "Mongrel."

"Who is Mongrel?"

"Really?" Bomber said.

"Shut up, Bomber, I've been through this all before. I'm done being screwed over. Answer the question, Dennis, or I'll put a full magazine from my Glock into your chest."

The big man glanced at Bomber. "Do it, Den. He means it. The guy took down some bent pigs a while back. He's capable."

"Mongrel is the president of the Taipans."

"Thank you."

The big man grunted.

"Where are you taking her?" I asked.

"Back to Dubbo and then to Sydney. We will escort her all the way. Her own personal bodyguards."

"Don't let me down, Dennis," I said to him, an edge to my voice. "I'd hate for something to happen to Helen."

"If anything does, it'll be over my dead body."

Looking into his eyes I could see that he meant it.

"Helen, you'll be fine," I said to her. She hugged me. "I believe him. He'll look after you."

"You have my word," Dennis said. He looked at his two henchmen. "Check outside."

They left the house while we finished discussing what would be done. A few minutes later, they came back in. "It's all good, Trench."

Trench? I didn't want to ask but felt compelled to. "Trench? Is there a reason they call you Trench?"

His head bobbed. "There is, but I'm not going to tell you. Give me your cell."

I handed it over, placing it into a plate-sized hand. Large fingers danced across the screen and then he handed it back. "The number I just put in there comes direct to me. Day or night."

"Thanks."

"You really need to put a PIN into that."

"Yeah."

Dennis turned to his friends. "Let's go."

Helen turned to me. "Mark?"

"You'll be fine. I promised, remember?"

I started to follow them towards the door. Dennis stopped me with a straight arm. "Stay in here. We'll take it now. She'll call you tomorrow night. Got it?"

"Take care of her, Dennis."

We had nothing. No leads, no witnesses—*Stan Collier!*

I was going to have to go out to Hampton and talk to him. But first I dialed Higgins. "I need some information."

"Good morning to you, too," he replied. He sounded tired.

"Long night?"

"Something like that. What can I do for you?"

"I've decided I'm not sitting around waiting for Agosti to come for me. I'm going to find him. He'll still be around here somewhere, so I need to find out where."

"I figured as much."

"I need some assurances just in case this shit goes south."

"Such as?" Higgins asked.

"Nicole being looked after along with Helen. And if I happen to put the bastard in the ground that there will be no repercussions."

"I think we might be able to arrange the first two. As for the third, I'm sure that if he did turn up dead, no one would investigate it over thoroughly."

"Good, now, have you any intel up your sleeve that I don't know about?"

"Nothing that will concern you," Higgins replied.

"What about the deaths of Franchi's men?"

"Nothing so far. No fibers, no prints. Not much at all."

"That doesn't help me much."

"Sorry, it's all I can do."

"Thanks."

The call ended. I was back to square one. Time to make another call.

"Yes?"

"I know who killed your men."

"Who?"

"Pete Agosti and his people."

"He's in Brunei," Franchi said.

Amazing what the criminal underworld knows. "No, he's in Australia. I found a drug lab he had set up. He's been supplying meth out here. The only problem is, he's disappeared."

"What do you want me to do about it, Mister Hayes?"

"I wasn't sure when I called but you knew he was in Brunei. I think you can find out where he might be."

"Why would I tell you now that I have the information I need?" he asked.

"Two reasons. One: You paid me to find whoever killed your people. Two: The cops are all over you at the moment. But I think you already know that."

"They will get bored with it."

"And Agosti will get away."

"Why are you pushing me hard on this?" the mobster inquired.

"Because it's personal."

"The policewoman?"

"Something like that."

"Give me a couple of hours and I'll see what I can find out."

Stan Collier slammed the door in my face. It didn't help much because I kicked it in anyway. It slammed back and the knob punched a hole in the asbestos wall lining.

"What are you doing?" he blurted out. "Get out of my home."

"Not until I get some answers."

"You put the cops on me," he shouted.

"You did that to yourself." I stalked towards him, causing him to backpedal. "Tell me more about the men who paid you."

"I already told you—"

My fist hit him in the face. I'm not normally a violent man but one can only take so much bullshit before he gets the urge to punch someone in the face

Collier sat down hard. I stood over him, my face full of menace. "Listen, my partner was shot, so was a fr—colleague, also someone I had helping me was murdered. Add into it the fact that the life of a young girl hangs on it, and it all comes down to one pissed off private investigator. Now, I know about the farm they were using, but what I want to know is if they mentioned anywhere else?"

Collier's eyes flickered.

"What did they say, Stan?"

"One of them mentioned something about a safe house."

I was getting angry again. "Do the police know?"

"No."

"Then why the bloody hell didn't you mention it?"

"These aren't people you mess with, mate. Agosti is a—"

He stopped, realizing he'd said too much.

Suddenly his arm flew behind him, but I was too quick. My Glock came out before his own weapon. I squeezed the trigger and the bullet punched into the floor beside him. Collier flinched.

"Let it go, Collier, or the next one goes into your guts."

The weapon hit the floor with a thud. "Shit."

"So, you work for Pete Agosti, huh?" I asked. It was more of a rhetorical question.

"No."

"Don't lie to me, Stan. Where might I find him?"

"I don't know."

The man was scared. "Safe house. Where is it?"

"I don't—"

I kicked him. He cried out in pain.

Moving into position for another go he said hurriedly, "Porter Creek. They set one up there."

"Where?"

"I don't know, honest. They just wanted me to do the car thing."

"Why Porter Creek?"

"I don't know," he replied.

"Who gave you the money? What was his name?"

"A big guy. Real big."

"Name, Stan. Give me a damn name."

"His friend called him Dennis."

Fuck me!

CHAPTER EIGHTEEN

I was a stupid, stupid man. I had pushed the thought of Bomber being involved out of my head and now it had come back to bite me on the ass. As I drove, I started to piece it all together. Dennis and his friends had shot at me when Nicole was hit. Bomber had staged his own shooting, as well as giving me just enough information without giving me too much. He hadn't seen anyone on the hill the day we drove past; the bastard knew they were there. Then he called in Dennis when I needed help for Helen. He was working with Agosti. The Taipans weren't involved. Just these bastards.

My foot went further to the floor and the needle came up to one-twenty. It was all the speed I could coax out of the Land Cruiser, and it seemed painfully slow.

My cell rang and I picked it up. "Yeah?"

"It me," said Franchi.

"Did you find something?"

"Yes, he's in Melbourne. Word is he's doing business while waiting for a package before leaving the country again."

"Any idea what the package is?"

"No."

It had to be Helen.

"Thanks."

So, this is the situation. I have two, possibly three different crews trying to kill me. Although I'm reasonably sure that Dennis and his friends, along with Bomber, were responsible for the initial shooting. Agosti was back cooking meth. Again, I'm sure that Bomber and his mates were up to their armpits in that as well. Bomber wormed his way in to my investigation; my fault there. He staged his own shooting and after Helen reappeared with the news that Agosti was her father, Bomber called in Dennis to keep her safe, to whom I handed Helen over and into Agosti's hands. Higgins was inside my head, saying *I told you so.* I would worry about the rest later.

Confused?

I wasn't. I was bloody pissed, and as I hit the outskirts of Friar's Lake, the Land Cruiser was still doing one-twenty. It was time to start breaking the branches off the tree one-by-one.

The Land Cruiser shuddered to a halt outside of Nicole's, stopping beside the police vehicle Jace was driving. I climbed out and he glared at me. "What the hell, Mark?"

"Inside, now."

Bomber was gone, Timmins lay on the floor, his head split open. I checked his pulse and found it beating strongly. "He's still alive."

"I'll call an ambulance and then you can tell me what's happening."

"I can't stay, Jace, I need to go."

He looked at me, incredulous. "What? No, you aren't leaving."

"Jace, I'll tell you everything when I get back. But if you need to know anything, call Stewart Higgins on this number." I wrote it down on a piece of paper. "I believe he's an inspector or something. You know him, he was the guy who grilled me after the Agosti thing blew up."

"I know him."

"He'll explain everything."

"Mark—"

"I'm going, Jace. Just call Higgins. Tell him to get his ass back here."

I left him standing, waiting for the ambulance.

I killed the call before answering it. Higgins had been persistently trying to call me ever since I'd left Friar's Lake on my way to Porter Creek.

When I arrived, the sun was starting to go down. An orange hue hung in the western sky. A cacophony of parrot squawks greeted me from the trees as I climbed out of the Land Cruiser. The heat was leaving the day but there was still some life in it yet. I closed the door and the sound echoed along the vacant main street.

As I walked up onto the sidewalk the grit of decades crunched audibly beneath my boots. In front of me was a familiar sight. A store I had visited not long ago when I first arrived in Friar's Lake looking for a missing person.

I found Mildred Brown behind the counter, counting out the money from her cash drawer. She looked up and smiled. "Mark, how are you?"

"I've been better, Mildred. I need your help if that's all right?"

She gave me a puzzled look. "If I can."

"Is there anyone new in town?"

"New? In this place? No. No one comes—"

"Yes, there is." The man's voice cut across her answer.

I looked to the doorway which led out to the residence. Mildred's husband, Oliver, stood there. He was a thin man with gray hair and a mustache.

"Are you sure, Oliver?" his wife asked him.

"Yes, saw them the other day. Rough looking lot."

"Can you describe them?" I asked.

"Not really, but one of them was big, really big. I also saw that bloke from Friar's Lake with them."

"What bloke?"

"Bomber, I think they call him."

I nodded. "Yeah, that's him. Thanks."

Mildred looked concerned. "Mark, is everything all right?"

I gave her a wan smile. "Just stay inside for the evening, Mildred."

"OK. Be careful, Mark."

"I plan to be. Oliver, can you tell me where they are?"

"Over on Girder Street."

"Thanks."

I went outside and stood beside the Land Cruiser to make a call. The other end buzzed twice before a gruff voice said, "What are you up to?"

"I'm in Porter Creek. Long story short, you were right, I was wrong. Bomber Hansen is working with some associates of his. Not the Taipans as far as I know. They have Helen and I'm about to get her back. They have a safe house here and I'm just letting you know in case it all goes to shit."

"You mean further into the shit."

"You could look at it that way."

"You need to wait for backup," Higgins said.

"I can't. Agosti is in Melbourne waiting for them to

deliver Helen to him."

"What about Friar's Lake police?"

"They're busy. Like I said, I'm not waiting."

Higgins sighed. "Don't get yourself shot."

"You got my back on this?" I asked him.

"All the way."

"Thanks."

I found the house easily. I waited until dark to get close enough without being seen. The lights were on but there was something odd about them. They weren't bright enough and then I realized they weren't using power.

I left the rifle in the Land Cruiser. This would be up close and personal. A daunting thought when it came to Dennis's size.

I closed in on the house. Like a lot of others in Porter Creek I could see the outline of graffiti on the external walls and large holes even though it was dark.

Around the side I saw their vehicle and two motorcycles. Harleys if I had to guess. I knew there were at least four adversaries inside. I needed to get them outside. To do that, I needed a plan.

Reaching into my pocket I took out a book of matches. Oh yeah, right, I hear you say, how convenient. Well, one must remember that in the outback, the nights are cold and if you get stuck without warmth, then you're in trouble. Therefore, I carry matches. Always.

I crept over to the first bike and unscrewed the fuel cap. Then I took some long strands of dead grass, bunched them together, and stuffed them into the tank.

Once that was done, I took the cap off the other bike, and left it. Then I went back to the first bike and lit the grass.

Now, grass that is dead doesn't burn like a rag. It just ignites and goes up in a hurry. So, the only thing I could do was run. Which I did, very fast around the house, turning the corner as the first bike blew up.

The darkness turned orange as the fireball rose above the roof line. The sound echoed throughout the dying town, accentuated by the still night. The first boom was followed by the second. By that time, I was almost to the rear.

Both bikes were ablaze, and the SUV was also starting to burn. Not that I could see it.

By the time I reached the back door, I could hear shouts from out front. I tried the back door, and it swung inward with more than a little force behind it. I stepped inside, finding the laundry at the back. Not that there was anything there, that's just what the small room should be used for.

From there, I entered the kitchen. There was a kerosene lantern on the table surrounded by beer cans and cigarette packets beside an overflowing ashtray. What caught my eye was the open packet of hollow point bullets and a loaded magazine which, I assumed, found its home in an automatic weapon, most likely the one that had sprayed Nicole's place when they tried to kill me.

I brought the Glock up and proceeded into the hallway. I could still hear the voices from out front. They were swearing loudly now. I checked the first room on my left. The door opened and I stuck my head inside. It was empty. Then I tried the room on my right. It was locked, from the outside.

"Helen?" My voice was just above a whisper.

"Mark?"

My foot crunched against the door. The force of it vibrated through my body as the door itself refused to move and stood there, still closed, as though saying, *stuff you*. OK, just remember, this isn't the movies, not every hero is Arnold or Sly. Some are like me.

I kicked it again. This time it flew back and crashed against the wall. Standing in the middle of the room on the other side was Helen.

She rushed forward. I said, "We don't have time for that, we need to leave."

I ushered her towards the back door. As we passed through the kitchen, I stopped, picked up the kerosene lamp and smashed it against the wall. The flammable liquid splashed everywhere, the flame inside igniting it. Hungry flames started to lick the wall and spread fast.

I followed Helen out through the back door and stopped. There, standing in front of us was Bomber Hansen, gun in his hand. "Some blokes around the front aren't happy with you."

"I'll have to apologize to them later, I've got places to go."

"How did you find us?" he asked.

"Collier."

"Yeah, maybe we should have killed him after all."

"You certainly fooled me, Bomber. Here I was thinking you had nothing to do with it. The bullet wound was a good touch."

He shrugged. "Yeah, well, I figured that with me on the inside, then I could control the situation. Then the whole thing with Helen happened and it was time to get out. How's Timmins?"

"In hospital I should imagine." Did you kill the Moron kid?" I asked.

He shook his head. "No, that was Dennis."

"Bryce?"

"Dennis."

"What about the two Franchi men?"

Bomber nodded. "Yeah, that was me. When they

showed up in town, I figured that they were trying to cut in on the drug trade. Agosti gave the order, and I lured them out to Hampton. The rest was simple."

"So, you were running all this for Agosti?" I asked.

"Sure."

"How did you become involved, Bomber? I don't understand."

"Bryce was waiting for me when I got out of jail. He offered me the job. I needed the money, so I took it. Spent a month in Sydney working contacts to set it all up. Once it was ready to go, Agosti had one of his blokes purchase the farm. All I had to do then was ship everything in. Things were good, too, until you fucked it up."

"You did that all on your own when you tried to kill me and missed," I pointed out.

"Agosti's orders, again. But Dennis missed, got your woman. Agosti ordered it stopped then and there because the events were drawing way too much attention. I told him that leaving you alive was a wrong move. I knew your reputation and that you wouldn't stop. I was right."

"Did you rob the armored truck as well?"

He shook his head. "Nope, that wasn't us. Anything else you want to know before I kill you?"

"Only one thing, the undercover in Dubbo. You or Dennis?"

Bomber smiled. "That was me. Could smell the pig shit on him a mile away."

Suddenly his smile disappeared. I could see the orange light flickering on his face. Then he realized what was happening. The house was burning. He glared at me, but I was already moving. With my left hand I pushed Helen aside while my right came up with the Glock in it and fired.

CHAPTER NINETEEN

The first bullet hit Bomber in the chest. There was no time for a well-placed shot, just point, shoot, and hope.

The force of the bullet made him stagger. The weapon in his hand exploded but his shot buried into the hard-packed earth some five feet to my right. I had the opportunity to take my time and fire again. I did so but chose to shoot Bomber in the leg. Maybe his other wound would kill him. I guess we'd find out eventually.

I grabbed Helen by the hand. "Come on, let's go."

Then we started to run. Just as fast as we could.

Ten meters, twenty...gunfire cracking as it passed us. I pushed Helen to the ground and crashed down beside her. "Stay here until I lead them away. Then go to the store," I told her and scrambled away into a dark shadow.

"Give it up, Hayes," a voice shouted at me. "You can't get away."

I figured it was Dennis. I gripped the butt of the Glock and slipped further into the darkness.

"Give us the girl back and we'll let you go."

"Not going to happen," I called out to him.

The weapon opened fire again, the bullets cutting through a sparsely foliaged bush beside me. Keeping low, I moved further away from Helen. I stopped behind a tree. "You'll have to do better than that, you fat, lying prick."

More bullets, these closer than the last. As I moved this time, a fence loomed in front of me. An old mesh cyclone one which I leaped over and sought shelter from the vacant house on the other side.

I pressed my back against it and peered around the corner. I could see Dennis and his friends moving in my direction. I raised the Glock and fired low. I wanted them chasing me not going to ground.

It elicited the desired reaction, and they came at me, hard. But they were careless, and I brought the Glock up again and aimed at the shorter of the three figures. I fired twice and he let out a shout and fell.

"Dennis, I'm shot. The prick shot me."

The automatic weapon opened up again and bullets chewed into the side of the house. I slipped back along the wall and in the dappled moonlight I found the back-door. Trying the handle and finding it open, I went inside and screwed my nose up as the stench. Something had died in there and it was rank. My stomach lurched the further I went into the center of the house.

I found a place in the kitchen where I could shelter behind a counter. This would be where I'd make my stand.

I crouched low, trying to control my breathing. My heart pounded, the sound hammering loudly in my ears.

Nervousness coursed through my body, my hands trembling. Then I heard the first of them step inside and a sense of calmness washed over me.

"Christ, what frigging died in here?" I heard one of them say.

"Shut up, Frog," another voice hissed. Obviously, Dennis.

"Well, it bloody stinks."

"Shut up or I'll shoot you myself."

Footsteps. Soft, light. But the problem with old rundown houses, the floors have a lot of give in them and even just the slightest bit of weight can cause sound. Which is what happened. A light squeak of two boards slipping together.

I came up and blew off four rounds from the Glock.

A scream of pain told me I'd found a target. It wasn't the desired target but the second of Dennis's comrades was out of the fight. The problem being, Dennis still had the automatic rifle and he started shooting the shit out of the kitchen.

Bullets punched holes in cupboards and walls. The flash from the barrel lit the inside like fireworks flashing on New Year's Eve. Chunks of asbestos and asbestos dust rained down over me, going into my lungs with each breath. Great, now if a bullet didn't kill me, the asbestos fibers would.

I hugged the floor, hands over my head, while Dennis emptied the magazine of the weapon he was using. When the shooting stopped, it took me a few moments to realize that it had actually ceased.

Coming up from behind the destroyed counter, my ears still ringing, I think Dennis was actually surprised to see I'd survived his crazy onslaught. I know I was. Maybe I looked like a dark wraith rising to take his soul for his dastardly deeds.

That was the plan, anyway. Send him to Hell and let them sort him out down there.

I fired. Once...twice...three times. Each time I heard

the bullets hammer into his massive frame. Each time they did so he lurched but didn't go down. So, I tried a fourth bullet. One that wasn't there. The magazine was empty.

Now I was armed with an empty gun and faced with an enraged mountain of a man staggering towards me. So I did the only thing available to me. I turned and—

Fell over.

"Shit," I growled out loud as I scrambled back across the debris covered floor.

Dennis loomed over me like some giant grizzly about to fall upon its prey. I guess that's what scared me the most. If the bastard fell on me from that height, he'd dead set kill me when he landed.

"You're dead, motherfucker," his voice was a gurgle, and I guessed I had hit him in at least one of his lungs.

The big man lurched forward again, his steps heavy, leaden. I scrambled back further until my back bashed into cupboards behind me, halting my retreat.

"Now what are you going to do?" Dennis asked.

His voice was slicker, wetter. I couldn't see his face, but I imagine blood leaking from the corner of his mouth as his lungs slowly filled. He coughed violently.

"You don't sound so good, Dennis. Guess I hit you in a good spot. Maybe you ought to take a seat before you die on your feet."

"I don't have time to die."

It sounded like some corny line out of a movie, but the more I stared up at his darkened figure, the more I kind of believed it. He was hell bent on killing me and not even the three bullets I'd put into him were going to stop him.

He stood over me. And I looked up, waiting for him to do something. Then Dennis's hand opened, and he dropped the weapon he'd been holding. It clattered to the floor beside him.

"I don't feel so good," he muttered.

The big man fell to his knees in front of me. It wasn't light; the whole house seemed to shake from the impact as he went down. Dennis stayed there for a few more heartbeats before he toppled to one side and crashed onto the floor. "Damn asshole. You bloody killed me."

I sat there, looking at him. Feeling sorry, I said, trying to ease his transition into the afterlife, "You got what you deserved. Happy travels."

Then he died. The rattling deep in his chest stopped along with his breathing.

Climbing to my feet, I walked around the counter and knelt beside the man on the other side. He was dead, too. Obviously, he'd bled out onto the floor.

I went outside and found the third of the killers. This one was still alive. "You got to help me, man. I'm bleeding."

"I don't need to do shit," I replied. "For all I care, you can die here in the dirt."

"Don't leave me here. I'll die, I'll die."

"I'll tell you what, I'm going to make a phone call to the police. It'll probably take them about 40 minutes to get here. If you live that long, it's a bonus. If you don't, I guess you got what you deserved."

"You're a cold-hearted bastard, Hayes."

"You shouldn't have shot my missus. You're lucky I haven't put a bullet in your head already."

I left it at that and went to find Helen.

She was waiting for me in the Land Cruiser.

"Are you alright?" I asked her.

"I think so. Is it over?"

"For the moment. I just have to make a phone call."

I took the cell out of my pocket, dialed in the number.

Higgins answered two rings later. "Do I take this as a good sign?" he asked.

"Depends if you call four down a good sign," I replied.

"Bloody shit, Mark, what did you do? Have a war out there or something?"

"Or something. You said you'd have my back on this. Is that true?"

"Yes, just get out of there. Did you get the girl back?"

"She's right here with me."

"What are you going to do with her?" Higgins asked.

"I have a plan. I'll be back in a couple of days. Just so you know, it was Bomber Hansen who killed your undercover in Dubbo. It was Dennis who killed Bryce. Bomber also killed the two Franchi men."

"Fill me in when you get back. But no longer than two days. I need you here so I can sort this shit out. Understood?"

"Yeah, got it."

"I don't believe it," Helen said. "You, a father?"

"What is so hard to believe?" I asked her indignantly.

"You're you, you just don't fit the mold."

"I agree," Nicole said.

"Don't you start." She looked well, mending terrifically. We'd been in Sydney for a day, and this was the first visit we'd made to the hospital. I'd arranged to meet Linda there, too. I had a feeling I was going to need a good lawyer.

Nicole stared at me. "Mark, are you going to tell me what's going on?"

"Soon, when Linda gets here."

"Why Linda?"

"She's a lawyer."

Nic rolled her eyes. "Shit, Mark, what have you done?"

"Should I leave now?" I turned and saw Linda standing in the doorway. "If I come in, I have a feeling I'm going to regret it."

She entered the room anyway and kissed Nicole on the cheek. She glanced at Helen and asked, "Who is this?"

"Her name is Helen," Nicole said.

"A stray?" Linda asked.

"I think I'd rather be a stray than stuck up," Helen shot back at her.

I grinned; this was going to be good if allowed to run its course. Linda pursed her lips. "No manners either."

"And you have no filter."

Suddenly Linda grinned. "I like her. Where did you find it?"

"She found me; her father is Pete Agosti."

"I knew I should have left."

"Are you serious?" Nicole asked incredulously.

"Afraid so."

"OK, that's it. You start talking right now and don't leave anything out."

My hand dipped into my pocket. It came back out with a twenty. I held it out to Helen. "Go get something to eat and drink from the cafeteria. It's on the second floor."

She nodded and took the money.

Once she was gone, I started from the beginning, leaving nothing out.

A heavy silence hung in the room when I was finished. I could see Linda wanted to run away and hide but Nicole was angry. With me, with the situation, with what could happen.

"You killed four men?" Linda asked, finding her voice.

"Two, technically. I'm not sure about the others. I haven't talked to Higgins to confirm it."

"I'm going to kick that prick in the nuts," Nicole growled. "How could he get you into something like this?"

"He didn't, Nic. They did when they tried to kill me and shot you. It was always going to end like this."

"You sure are in the middle of a shit sandwich, aren't you?" Linda said.

"That's why you are here. Just in case. I think Higgins is a man of his word, but you never know."

"You just had to screw up my town while I wasn't there," Nicole growled at me.

"I tried hard not to." I was still sitting on the armored truck robbery. Maybe that could wait until I'd looked into it further.

"What about the girl?" Linda asked. "What do you plan on doing with her?"

"I need somewhere for her to go in the short term," I replied. I let my gaze linger on Linda until my telepathic thoughts finally cracked her concrete façade.

"No." She shook her head. "Not going to happen."

"It won't be for long. Just until her father is either picked up or out of the picture."

"Mark—"

"She's got nowhere else. At the moment I'm still a target."

"Surely there is somewhere more suitable. What happens to her when it's all over?"

I looked at Nicole. "I thought—"

Her face told the story. "Oh, Mark, she can't stay with us."

"She trusts me—us," I pointed out. "Her mother is most likely dead, and her father responsible."

"Mark, what about our baby?"

"We can all live together, Nic. It's not like she's a small child. She's almost an adult."

"I don't know, Mark."

"Just think about it. She'll be able to help around the house while you recuperate. In the meantime…"

I turned my gaze on Linda.

She sighed. "All right, I suppose I can keep an eye on her for a couple of days."

"Thank you."

Helen arrived back with some kind of salad in a Styrofoam container and a water. She said to me, "You owe me five dollars."

"What? I gave you twenty."

"It doesn't go far in this place."

I reached into my pocket and took out my wallet. I opened it and retrieved $200. "Take this. It'll see you through for the next few days."

"Two days, Mark," Linda reminded me.

Helen frowned. "What's going on?"

"You're going to stay with Linda for a few days."

Linda glared at me. "*Two* days, Mark."

"Well, what do you say?"

Helen shrugged. "I suppose it'll be all right."

"Fine. I need to go."

Nicole glared at me once more. "Where?"

"Back to Friar's Lake. I have to see Higgins."

"Can't you stay?"

"No, sorry."

"Then be careful."

"Aren't I always?"

"About time you got back," Higgins said to me. Such and Waters were in the interrogation room. Such stared at me with displeasure.

She said, "If it was up to me, you would be rotting in a jail cell."

"Did you explain everything to her?" I asked Higgins.

"Some."

"Not the part where they killed an undercover, and the Moron kid?"

She turned her head and looked glaringly at Higgins. Obviously not. "Where do you want me to start?" I asked him.

"How about the beginning."

So, once more I told the story.

"Why didn't you wait for backup?" Such asked.

"There was no time. They could have shifted her without any notice."

"Bomber Hansen survived, by the way," Higgins informed me. "He's in Dubbo hospital under armed guard. He'll be charged with murder later today."

"What about the others?"

"All dead."

"Oh well."

"Is that all you've got to say?" Such hissed.

"Ease it down a bit, Such," Higgins said. "We're just here to get the story straight."

"And then let him walk."

Higgins nodded. "That's right. He was working for me. Anything that he did was sanctioned and that is it. There is nothing else."

"What about Agosti?" I asked Higgins.

"We've passed on what we know to Victoria Police. They'll take it from there with help from the Feds."

"So you have no idea where he is."

"No."

"There might be one more thing," I said.

They looked at me.

I dug into my pocket and took out the bill with the dye on it. "I believe this came from the armored truck heist."

"What?" Such blurted out.

"I picked it up the other day. I wasn't sure so I looked into it some before coming to you." I could see the anger in her eyes now. "The lass at the roadhouse received it off a bloke called Gerald Long. He lives out at Old Dog Flats."

"Is the girl willing to testify that is who she got it from?" Such asked.

"I believe she will."

"You do realize that he could have got it from anywhere," Waters said to me.

"He could have but I believe he's part of a local crew. Tom Mason, Gerald Long, Jimmy Morrison, Betty Mason. Maybe some others."

"You should be telling this to the Serious Crimes boys," Higgins said.

"It's not confirmed. Just a hunch. All I'm saying is that they might look into them. Tom Mason served in the Army. He could have trained them."

Such said, "How about you leave it to the professionals. I was talking to the Crime Squad boys yesterday and they believe that a professional team came in specially for the job before leaving."

I shook my head and looked at Higgins. "They're wrong."

"Like she said, leave it to them."

"All right, fine. I'll just go back to doing what I was doing."

"That would be a good idea."

And it probably would have been. But I did, and it led me into more trouble.

CHAPTER TWENTY

Old Dog Flats was pretty much just that. Flat. How the hell are you supposed to sneak up on a place when everything for miles around it was like a billiard table? You make out you're someone you are not.

Hence, I drove up to the main house and pretended I was from the Department of Primary Industries investigating the wild dog problem in the district.

I eased the Land Cruiser to a stop and climbed out. A young man with a solid build and dark hair and eyes came out of a machinery shed, grease covering his arms and hands. "Something I can do for you, mate?"

"My name is Mark Xavier. I'm from the DPI. I'm out in the district looking into the wild dog problem."

"Oh, yeah?"

I nodded. "You been having any problems with them at all?"

"Nothing I can't handle," he replied.

"I didn't catch your name."

"Gerald Long."

I held out my hand. "Pleased to meet you, Gerald. You work this place on your own?"

He held up a greasy hand and shrugged. "Drought. Have to to make ends meet. Ain't got enough money to hire anyone at the moment."

I nodded. "Right. How is it that you handle the wild dogs?"

"I've got a rifle and sometimes I use baits."

"Do you have permits for the baits?" I asked him.

He nodded. "Sure, they're inside."

"Would you mind if I had a look at them?"

"I'll have to go and get them."

"That's OK, I'll wait."

He turned away and walked towards the house. I waited until Long was out of sight and walked over to the machinery shed and looked inside.

Surprise, surprise, he was working on a prime mover. I hurriedly dug into my pocket for my cell and called Jace. "Mark? What's—"

"What color was that prime mover that was involved in the armored truck heist?"

"Dark blue, why?"

"Was it a Mack?"

"Yes."

"Thanks," I replied and disconnected.

I walked around to the front of the truck. The hood was up, and the bull bar was pointed at the ground, but I could see the damage on it. I took a couple of pictures and kept looking. I opened the passenger door.

I don't know what I expected to find. And I found about that much. Nothing.

Closing the door, I walked back around the front towards the door.

"Are you right there or what?"

I froze. Gerald Long had been quicker than I figured. My brain ticked over as I tried to come up with a reason I was snooping around. Smiling, I said, "Sorry, you caught me snooping. I have a thing for farm machinery sheds. It's amazing what old equipment you find in them. Some farmers hold onto stuff that date back to the twenties. Amazing."

He looked skeptical. "Oh, yeah. Well, you won't find any of that shit in here."

"Shame."

He held out the paperwork he had in his hand. I took it and looked it over, making sure he wasn't trying to catch me out.

Passing them back, I said, "Looks OK to me. Have you been getting many?"

"Two last week. There are still a few more out there."

It was time for me to go. "OK, well, I must move on. Thanks for taking the time to talk. I'll see you next time I'm around."

"The next time?"

"Sure. While we're still getting reports I'll be around occasionally."

"Fair enough."

I climbed into the Land Cruiser and felt a wave of relief wash over me as I started the motor. As I left the yard I looked into my mirror and saw him take out a cell and make a call. I think I may have rattled his cage.

When I got back to Nicole's, I found Betty Mason on the lounge. She wore a pair of tight jeans and a white tank top with no bra beneath it, so her nipples stabbed against the stretchy fabric, pushing it out. She had a seductive look about her, something akin to a female praying mantis right before the male copulates with her as she contemplates which part of your head will taste the best.

"How did you get in here?" I asked her, instantly becoming wary.

"Is that any way to greet someone who is about to rock your world?" she asked.

Rock my world? Chew me up and spit me out more like it. "What can I do for you, Betty?"

She got up off the sofa and walked past me and into the kitchen. I followed her and watched as she opened the refrigerator and took out two beers. She cracked the lid off the first bottle and passed it to me. "Beer?"

I took it. "Sure, why not. Don't mind if I have one of my own. Feel free to have one yourself."

"Thank you."

She cracked hers and walked over to me. When she stopped, her nipples were so close it felt as though they were about to pierce my chest. She casually took a mouthful and swallowed. "Do you think I'm attractive, Mark?" she asked. I could smell the beer on her breath.

Every nerve ending was tingling throughout my body. "Yes, ah…sure."

She leaned in closer to whisper into my ear. "Then fuck me, Mark. Take me into the bedroom and make me do things to you that I wouldn't normally do. I'd like that. Hit me, Mark, hit me."

"No."

Her hand shot out like a striking snake. Her open palm striking me across my cheek. It stung, but it wasn't enough to really hurt. I was shocked more than anything.

I looked into Betty's eyes; the lust was there, a smoldering fire. She smiled. "Hit me, Mark."

"No."

Her hand shot out again, this time it was harder. "Come on, Mark, hit me. You know you want to."

"No."

This time she hit me with a closed fist and before I

knew what was happening, my own hand shot out as I gave her a solid backhand. Betty's head snapped to one side before she turned it back to stare at me, her eyes sparkling with desire, blood at the corner of her mouth.

Suddenly she lunged at me, pressing her lips against mine. I grabbed her arms and tried to push her away but as I did pain seared through my bottom lip as she bit down hard upon it.

I pulled back, the coppery taste of blood filling my mouth. Betty licked the blood off her lips and her smile widened. "Did you like that? Did it make you hard?"

I wiped the blood away, pain making my lip tingle. "Betty, what are you doing?"

Her nipples seemed to be harder, larger than what they had been before, if it was at all possible. "I thought that was obvious, Mark. I want you for myself. Give that cow the ass and you can have me. Shit, you can have me anyway."

"No, Betty. Nic and me are going to have a baby."

"You can have me, Mark." Betty took her tank top off revealing her almost perfect breasts.

I closed my eyes, not wanting to stare at them. "You had better go, Betty."

I heard her sigh. "I'm sorry, Mark."

My eyes flashed open. "What—"

Then my head started ringing as I collapsed to my knees. My vision blurred and I heard Betty's voice in the distance say, "No, keep him alive. I want to see if he will change his mind."

"Christ, Betty, let's just kill him." Tom Mason. "He knows everything."

"No, we do as I say."

As darkness engulfed me, I realized that I had it all wrong. Tom Mason wasn't the one behind the robbery of the truck. It was Betty.

I woke up with a hand rubbing at my crotch and a voice said, "Shit, Betty, do you think sex is the answer to everything?"

"It worked for you, Tom," I heard her say.

"I still think we should just kill him."

"You already tried that twice and it didn't work. Now we'll try my way. If it doesn't work, then you can kill him."

"I think he's hot." A different female voice. Possibly Nellie Brown.

"You're like Betty, Nellie. You'd screw anything that moved." Bluey Timms?

"He knows about the truck." Gerald Long.

All that was missing— "You shouldn't have left him alone." Jimmy Morrison.

The gang's all here.

I groaned, letting them think I was starting to wake. Not that it was hard to groan; my head hurt like a bitch and Betty was still rubbing at my hardening member. "That—that's one way to wake up," I said croakily.

I opened my eyes and could see I was strung up by my hands in a machinery shed. They all gathered around me in a semicircle. "I'm sorry that Tom had to hit you, Mark," Betty said. "I wish there could have been another way."

"So, what now?" I asked.

"That's up to you."

I looked around the gathering. Apart from Betty and Nellie, the rest stared daggers at me. I mean, Nellie was staring at me, with her blue eyes. But I think by the time the blonde with the lithe body diverted her gaze I was totally undressed.

"How did you eventually work out it was us?" Tom asked.

"First was the fact you paid your debt," I explained. "I wasn't totally sold on the idea but then a banknote with dye on it turned up at the roadhouse. Gerald passed it over."

All eyes turned in Gerald Long's direction. "You stupid prick," Morrison growled.

I left out the part about telling the police.

"It's too late to worry about it now," Betty said.

"Did you tell the police?" Tom Mason asked.

"No."

"Are you sure?"

"Do you think I would be out at Gerald's place if I told the police?" I asked him.

"All right. We kill him, Betty." A handgun came free of his belt, and I recognized it as my Glock.

"Whoa, just slow it down a bit," I blurted out.

"Wait," Betty said stepping in front of me. "If he is to die then I will tell you. Everybody out."

"Betty—" Tom started.

"Out!"

Everyone turned and left except Tom. "I don't like it, Betty."

"It's fine. Go. Get ready."

Tom left and Betty turned to me. I said, "I'm not going to sleep with you, Betty."

She pouted at me. "Pity. But never mind. I will give you a choice. You help us or I will let Tom kill you."

"Help you with what?" I asked.

"Another robbery."

"Killing a guard wasn't enough last time? You're going back for more?"

"That wasn't meant to happen. It was his own fault."

"Meant or not, the bloke is still dead. You were lucky

it wasn't two. Killing a man is a long way from stealing a bull and milking it. Mind you, I bet you've milked a few in your time."

Betty smiled at the barb. "What's it going to be, Mark? You joining us, or dying?"

"I don't see that I have much choice, do I?"

She shook her head. "No."

"When is it happening?" I asked Betty after she let me down.

"Tomorrow. The armored truck will be headed south after doing a pickup in Friar's Lake."

"Not much money coming out of the bank there," I pointed out.

"Silly. It does a circuit. Friar's Lake will be the last stop before it heads to Dubbo."

"How are we doing it?" I asked. "The same as last time?"

"Similar."

"What do you want to know for?" Tom Mason asked. "Just keep to yourself, Hayes. I don't trust you. If you step out of line, one of us will put a bullet in your head."

I stared at him. "If I'm going to be part of this, I want to know what's going to happen."

"You'll be told last minute."

For the rest of the day, we hung around in the machinery shed. Then as the sun was going down, everyone got their swags out of their vehicles and lay them out inside. "What's going on?" I asked Betty.

"We all stay here before we do the job."

Shit, they were sounding like hardened criminals. "What do we do for food?"

Betty looked at Bluey Timms. "What do we have?"

"I have some frozen meals in the freezer."

So, we were at Bluey Timms's place. Wherever that was.

"Take Nellie and organize something to eat for us. After we eat, Gerald and Jimmy can go and get the truck."

While they went and got food, I sat by myself contemplating how the hell I was going to get out of the predicament I found myself in.

Movement brought me awake. It was faint but close by. "Don't make a sound," Nellie Brown said to me as she slipped under the blanket with me. The dark shed was lit by the orange light of a kerosene lamp.

I opened my mouth to speak when I felt the sharp sting from the point of a knife. My lips snapped shut firmly.

"There, isn't that better?" she asked.

"Only if you're on the other end of the knife."

"Poor baby. Take off your pants."

"I already told Betty I wasn't going to sleep with her. How do you think she'll take me sleeping with you?"

"I'd say not well."

We both looked over at Betty. She looked displeased. "Nellie, what are you doing?"

"Just having some fun."

"If you want to have some fun, try one of the boys. I'm sure they're wound up just as much as you are."

Nellie climbed out from under the blanket. I looked over at Betty. "Thank you."

"Don't thank me. If I can't have you, she sure as shit can't."

I went back to sleep, only to be woken by a boot to the ribs just after first light. "Get up."

I stared at Tom Mason who stood menacingly over me. "Good morning to you, too."

"You're driving the truck."

"What?"

"You're driving the truck. Gerald will be in there with you. Try anything smart and he'll kill you."

"What am I supposed to do with the truck?"

"Watch and learn." He turned and said, "Everyone gather around."

Once the crew were all together, Betty took over. "Right, we set up the roadblock here, at the intersection. The truck hits them like last time." She looked at me. "Hit them hard. That armored truck has to go over."

I waited for them to continue.

"The getaway vehicle, should we need it, will be occupied by Nellie and Bluey. Jimmy, I, and Tom will take the armored truck. Gerald will stand guard. Mark will remain in the truck until the job is done and then we all meet back here."

Tom shook his head. "No. Hayes gets out and gets his hands dirty."

Betty nodded. "All right. Everyone don't worry about masks. We leave soon. If the truck is on time we need to be in place."

"Why don't we need masks?" I asked out loud.

Tom said, "You won't need one because there won't be any witnesses."

My blood ran cold. That was it. They meant to kill everyone and possibly me when it was over. Tom smiled as he realized that I'd put it together.

There was only one thing for it, I had to figure out how I was going to get out of it.

CHAPTER TWENTY-ONE

Gerald Long was careless. When he'd fixed the truck, he'd left a screwdriver in a position where it wasn't obvious except when you climbed into the cab of the prime mover. Things were looking up after all.

It cost him his life.

Something I'd have to answer for later on. However, with his death came the advantage of accessing his cell phone.

How did it happen?

Like this.

We were driving along the highway following the other two vehicles. I had managed to sequester the screwdriver on my person without Gerald seeing. Then slowly we dropped back some distance behind the others.

"You need to speed up," he said to me.

"I would but there seems to be a warning light on, and the revs won't come up," I lied.

He frowned. "Where?"

"Can't you see it?"

"No."

"It's right there," I said, nodding at the dash.

He leaned over and then I struck. The screwdriver came up and swept across as I gritted my teeth and drove it into his throat.

I won't describe how he died, let's just say it wasn't pretty and leave it at that. However, as I drove, I managed to get his cell and the seatbelt managed to keep him erect.

I dialed.

"Such."

"Listen to me. There's going to be another truck heist this morning."

"Really?"

"Yes, really. On the highway headed south," I explained. "At one of the intersections."

"Which one?"

"I don't know, they didn't tell me."

"Hayes, we don't have time for this."

My anger rose. "Damn it, Such, I'm driving the fucking truck."

"That's it, goodbye."

She hung up. For a moment I was stunned. The silly cow hung up on me and now in front of me, the vehicles were slowing down at a crossroads. The ambush site.

It was a normal looking crossroads. The highway running north-south with the other running northeast-southwest. Both had stop signs on them. There were some trees in one of the paddocks, but most were bare.

Tom Mason directed me to the right. I indicated, took the turn, and then drove along it for a distance before I could turn around.

When I stopped, I pulled off the road and waited. My mind whirled as I tried to figure out the next part of my plan. I didn't have one. Such had killed that.

I looked over at Gerald Long and said, "Any ideas?"

He said nothing. Strange that.

"Gerald, are you there?"

Bloody hell—he had a Walkie Talkie on him. I leaned over to find it.

"Gerald are you there?"

Shit, it was in his pocket. I fumbled it out and then said, "Here."

There was a pause and for a moment I thought maybe I'd been rumbled. Then, *"Is everything all right?"*

"Yes."

It went quiet after that. For a further twenty minutes I thought that nothing was going to happen. Maybe Such had tipped off the truck and they had rerouted. If that was the case, where were the police? Then in the shimmering distance of the morning heat, I saw the truck appear at the end of a long straight.

"Get ready."

Through the front windscreen I saw the blocking vehicle move. It stopped halfway across the intersection and then Tom climbed out with his weapon. The hood went up and he pretended to be working on it. Jimmy and Betty crouched on the blind side of the parked vehicle.

I turned the motor over and it came to life. Across the way I could see the vehicle Nellie was driving, Bluey in the passenger seat. I had no doubt that the motor was running in it as well.

The armored truck grew nearer and as it did, I could see it slowing. They were going to stop. I could hear myself whispering urgently to tell it to keep going but alas to no avail.

"Move now," I heard Betty say over the walkie talkie.

I glanced over at Gerald. "Well, I guess I can't let her down."

I let out the clutch and started moving forward. Working my way through the gears I was soon moving at a good clip. By the time I reached the crossroads something strange was happening. The rear door on the armored truck was flung open and armed police officers were climbing out.

Surprised, Tom, Betty, and Jimmy Morrison had their automatic weapons up and were moving like a well-oiled machine. Tom had trained them well.

I saw a police officer go down and hoped like hell it wasn't one of the ones from Nicole's crew.

Ahead of me I saw Jimmy work his way around the front of the blocking vehicle. His weapon was up, and he was spraying gunfire towards the rear of the armored truck. Before I knew what was happening, my foot went down further on the gas pedal, and I turned the wheel slightly to make an adjustment to my course.

Before anyone knew what was happening, the truck crashed into the blocking vehicle like a runaway locomotive. Somewhere in between both was Jimmy Morrison, the impact turning him into mush.

The truck plowed on, shoving the blocking vehicle violently aside. The side window shattered as bullets punched through it. I glanced out at Tom Mason, a snarl of rage on his face. Then he was gone.

I wasn't sure where Betty was. I didn't see her. What I did see, however, was the getaway vehicle with Nellie and Bluey coming towards the intersection. Suddenly they stopped.

Nellie reversed, swinging on the wheel. She was trying to turn. They were going to run. My foot went all the way to the floor. Black smoke belched from the twin exhausts of the prime mover.

The vehicle disappeared beneath the front of the truck and almost immediately I felt the beast shudder with the impact.

I stamped on the brakes and the prime mover jerked

to a halt. I climbed down from the cabin and walked around to the front. The getaway vehicle was a crumpled mess. Bluey Timms's head rested on the dash, eyes open, blood running from various cuts and gashes. Beside him, Nellie looked just as battered from the impact. The only difference, she was still alive. She moaned; bloody drool spilled from her open mouth.

"You fucking asshole!"

I turned and saw Betty Mason standing there, hands full of weapon. There were tears in her eyes, spilling down her cheeks. Blood ran from a gash in her left arm, no doubt clipped by a bullet. But she also had other cuts and grazes from where I'd crashed through their roadblock.

"It's over, Betty," I told her. "It's over."

"It will be when I kill you," she hissed.

I held up a hand in a defensive gesture. "No, Betty, wait!"

I was dead, there was no doubt about it. Betty was going to kill me and there was nothing I could do. But instead of killing me, she died.

Three bullets. Three bullets fired rapidly from a handgun snuffed out her young life. One…two…three. Two in the torso, one in the head. Betty Mason collapsed to the asphalt and leaked blood onto the already burning hot blacktop.

I stared at her in horror. Sure I'd killed before, but seeing Betty shot down like that in front of me does things to one's brain. Therapy coming up.

"Are you alright?"

I looked up and saw Such standing there, vest on, her handgun still ready to go. "I'm fine."

"Stay here."

She disappeared and I realized that there was still

gunfire happening. Then there wasn't, and it all went quiet.

I walked around the prime mover and stared at the carnage in front of me. Two officers were down as well as the last of the robbers, Tom Mason. People were shouting and running and trying to help the wounded. It was chaos.

It was over.

The end tally was one police officer killed, one wounded, five robbers dead, and Nellie Brown in a coma and unexpected to live out the week. It was a terrible result. The police officer who'd been killed was a young detective constable from the Crime Squad. The wounded officer was Jace. He'd been hit in the leg but would mend with time.

"How are you doing?" Higgins asked me.

I looked up from the coffee cup. Such stood beside him. I nodded. "I'll be fine."

"You were lucky."

"Maybe."

"That crazy bitch would have killed you if I hadn't seen her," Such said.

She had a point there.

"How did you end up with them, anyway?" Higgins asked.

"I was kidnapped."

Higgins sighed. "Start at the beginning."

Once I was finished Higgins shook his head. "You're a trouble magnet, Hayes."

"Well, you people wouldn't believe me, so, I had to do it myself."

Such looked at Higgins. "What do we do? Arrest him or let him go?"

"Let him go. If anyone asks, he was working for me as a paid informant. Better still, just direct them to me and I'll field any questions."

I said, "You know, they were going to kill all the armored truck guards, right? And me as well."

They nodded.

"Is everything sorted with the money?" I asked them. "The stuff in Nicole's bank?"

Higgins said, "Yes, I saw to it myself."

"Thank you."

"Don't leave town for a few days, just in case I need to speak to you."

"You'll have to do it over the phone. I'm going to Sydney."

"Fine, I can do that. Anything to add, Such?"

She looked at me before finally saying, "Stay out of trouble, Hayes. Please, stay out of trouble."

I left the station and once outside, my cell rang. I answered it, listened for a moment and then disconnected. I needed to go to Melbourne instead.

The Audi eased to a stop and the headlights went out. Three men climbed from the vehicle and moved to stand in front of it.

"You don't have to do this, Mark," Tia said to me. It was one time that I was more than happy to have my ex-wife with me.

I looked at her. "If this goes bad, Tia, put them down."

"I promise."

I climbed out and closed the door. I'd switched the

interior light off so they couldn't see who was in the car with me. I walked forward and stopped.

"I got your message. What do you want?"

I stared at Agosti, taking a moment before I spoke. "Your daughter."

"What about her?"

"I want you to leave her alone. Let her come to live with me."

Agosti chuckled. "Why would I do that? What I should do is just kill you, get rid of my problems altogether."

For a moment I thought it was a cue for his men to act but the construction site where we had met remained silent. I said, "You can't take her on the run with you. The cops know where you are, and you can bet it won't be long until they try to sweep you up. Besides, the girl will only resent you because you killed her mother."

The remark elicited more laughter. "That's what you think? The silly cow got stoned and left. I have no idea where she is, but dead she isn't."

"What's your answer, Pete?" I asked. "Are you going to let Helen come and live with me or are we going to war over her, because I'm not letting her go with you. One of us will die and I'm almost certain it won't be me."

"You got balls, Hayes, I'll give you that. Maybe Helen needs something like that in her life." He paused and then shrugged his shoulders. "All right, Hayes. We'll do it your way. She can stay with you and your copper."

Relief. "There is one more thing, Pete. You don't come back. She's better off without you. You stay away."

"What if I don't?"

"Then we're back at square one and all bets are off."

Another moment of silence. "All right, Hayes. But you look after her or the shoe will be on the other foot."

"I'll look after her better than you can, Pete."

He nodded and turned away, his men following him. They climbed back into the Audi and the motor started.

The headlights came on and for a moment I was blinded. Then the car turned around and disappeared into the night.

I climbed back into the car I'd been driving. Tia said, "That looked intense."

"Yeah. But it worked out. Looks like I just became Helen's guardian."

"Good luck with that," Tia said grimly.

I opened the door and stepped back, allowing Nicole to walk through the doorway followed by Helen. Nic stood in the middle of the living room and took a deep breath. "It's good to be home," she said as she breathed out.

"Sit down, and take it easy," I said to her. "Put your feet up."

Nicole did as I said and then Helen sat in one of the armchairs. "This is a nice place."

"Treat it as home," Nicole said to her. "If you need anything, just ask."

I said, "Tomorrow we'll go and see about school."

Helen screwed up her face. Typical teenager response. "You'll be fine."

There was a moment of silence before she asked, "Will he be back?"

I shook my head. "No. I don't think so. If he does, then we'll deal with it."

"I need clothes."

Nicole smiled. "I'll take you shopping tomorrow. We'll get you what you need."

"Nothing too revealing," I said firmly.

Helen rolled her eyes. "Really?"

"Pull your head in, Hayes," Nicole said to me. "Let me take care of this."

I shrugged. "All right."

Helen got to her feet. "I might go and check my room out."

Nicole said, "Down at the end of the hall on your right."

When Helen was gone, I walked over to the sofa and squished myself onto it. Nic giggled. "What are you doing?"

"I want to be close to my two favorite people."

"Really?"

"Yeah. I missed you, Nic. I was worried that I was going to lose you. But now you're here and it feels like everything is right in the world once again."

She kissed me on the lips. "We missed you, too."

I placed my head on her shoulder and closed my eyes. "Love you, Nic."

"Love you, too."

We stayed like that for another thirty seconds. Then my cell rang.

A LOOK AT: DEADLY WATER

FROM THE AUTHOR OF THE ACTION-PACKED TEAM REAPER SERIES COMES A NEW PAGE-TURNER YOU WON'T WANT TO PUT DOWN!

A car bomb in a quiet suburban street sets in motion an investigation which will uncover the tentacles of organized crime stretching from the water-starved outback to the halls of power in the country's capital.

Senator Colin Worth was about to introduce a water bill which would cost the big producers millions before he was assassinated. However, the trail—as investigated by Detective Sergeant Gloria Browning and her team—only throws up more questions than answers.

Meanwhile, former undercover operative Dave Nash is brought in to investigate the disappearance of a water inspector in the town of Collari, on the Barwon River. But things take an even darker turn when Gloria's daughter, Rachel, is abducted.

Now, to get her back, Nash has to go against an organization who feeds its victims to the trees.

AVAILABLE NOW

ABOUT THE AUTHOR

A relative newcomer to the world of writing, Brent Towns self-published his first book, a western, in 2015. *Last Stand in Sanctuary* took him two years to write. His first hard-cover book, a Black Horse Western, was published the following year.

Since then, he has written 26 western stories, including some in collaboration with British western author, Ben Bridges.

Also, he has written the novelization to the upcoming 2019 movie from One-Eyed Horse Productions, titled, *Bill Tilghman and the Outlaws*. Not bad for an Australian author, he thinks.

Brent Towns has also scripted three Commando Comics with another two to come.

He says, "The obvious next step for me was to venture into the world of men's action/adventure/thriller stories. Thus, Team Reaper was born."

A country town in Queensland, Australia, is where Brent lives with his wife and son.

In the past, he worked as a seaweed factory worker, a knife-hand in an abattoir, mowed lawns and tidied gardens, worked in caravan parks, and worked in the hire industry. And now, as well as writing books, Brent is a home tutor for his son doing distance education.

Brent's love of reading used to take over his life, now it's writing that does that; often sitting up until the small hours, bashing away at his tortured keyboard where he loses himself in the world of fiction.

www.ingramcontent.com/pod-product-compliance
Lightning Source LLC
La Vergne TN
LVHW030918080826
845145LV00013B/2958